KILL PETROSINO!

It is the turn of the century. Lieutenant Joe Petrosino of the New York Police Department is a man with an obsession. Believing that there is a secret society controlling organised crime in America, he aims to expose the Mafia. With disbelieving superiors, he alone must face the feared Don Vito Cascio Ferro. Would-be informers are too scared to talk, but Petrosino gets his first lead with the discovery of a brutally murdered body in a New York alley . . .

Books by Frederick Nolan
in the Linford Mystery Library:

THE OSHAWA PROJECT
NO PLACE TO BE A COP
SWEET SISTER DEATH

FREDERICK NOLAN

KILL PETROSINO!

Complete and Unabridged

LINFORD
Leicester

First published in Great Britain

First Linford Edition
published 2007

British Library CIP Data

Nolan, Frederick W., *1931 –*
 Kill Petrosino!.—Large print ed.—
 Linford mystery library
 1. Police—New York (State)—New York
 —Fiction 2. Mafia—New York (State)—New
 York—Fiction 3. Detective and mystery
 stories 4. Large type books
 I. Title
 823.9′14 [F]

ISBN 978–1–84617–950–1

Published by
F. A. Thorpe (Publishing)
Anstey, Leicestershire

Set by Words & Graphics Ltd.
Anstey, Leicestershire
Printed and bound in Great Britain by
T. J. International Ltd., Padstow, Cornwall

This book is printed on acid-free paper

1

Daily, at around eleven in the morning, work in Palermo comes slowly to a stop. Some people say that this habit is a throwback to Moorish times, a thousand years before the Normans came to plunge Sicily into the black pit of feudal night. Others, perhaps more worldly-wise, will tell you that it has grown out of the pleasure of the men in the darkly discreet clothes whom you will see in certain crowded cafés near the Quattro Canti, standing close together with just enough room to raise the tiny cups of *caffe solo* to unsmiling lips, talking in quiet voices beside the zinc-topped serving bars; cool and guarded men, watching nothing and seeing everything. But whether it be the preference of *mafiosi* or the pleasure of Sultans matters ultimately not at all, for the tradition, like all Sicilian traditions, is old-established and inimical to change. So, at around eleven each morning, the streets are redolent of fresh-ground coffee, and people move without haste in the sharp black shadows of the pink buildings, freed for a short while from whatever cares beset them.

Palermo might be called beautiful, but it is not pretty.

Despite the olive-groves and the almond trees, despite the heavy vines and the luxuriant gardens, and the dimpled statues of saints and Kings of Spain, there is still a Saracen harshness in the air. It is almost as if the very stones themselves offer a sullen resistance to the gentling hand of man, a stubborn opposition which seems to be reflected in the very way that Palermo itself is built.

The town lies in the crook of the arm of a rocky bay. At the northern end is Monte Pellegrino, at the south Cape Zafferano. The plain on which it stands — the Golden Conch Shell — rises through groves of palm, orchards of orange and lemon, to the bleak mountains beyond. The city lies there as though determined to be hospitable, although not wishing to. Where Naples smiles to welcome the arriving traveller, where Rome excites, where Milano challenges — Palermo simply is. You may come if you will. You may stay if you desire. You may return if you must. But when you are gone, stranger, you will be neither mourned nor missed. Unchangeable, unchanging, Palermo and her people say : we are what we are. It is not necessary that you like us. We would not ask it. We do not desire it.

The Birreria Italia, on the Via Roma not far from the Quattro Canti, was crowded, as always. Not because it was in any way different in its style or its furnishing from any of a dozen such cafés scattered along the city's littered main street. The popularity of the Italia was simply explained : here Don Vito Cascio Ferro took his morning coffee and here, because of that, any *mafioso* who happened to be in the capital would come by to pay his respects, to take a cup of Moretti's good coffee, perhaps talk shop awhile.

And naturally all those who wished to see or be seen by the *amici* gravitated to the same place at the same time. Suppliants, celebrity-spotters, would-be courtiers and hangers-on either real or otherwise crowded the tables inside.

For those who knew no better, there were tables on the pavement outside, but they were normally unoccupied except by *strabieri*, outsiders, tourists who only saw the crowd elbow-to-elbow all the way along the bar and took their coffee outside in the flat heat of the climbing sun or else — preferably — found somewhere less noisy.

Inside, the café was unremarkable. Along the left hand wall, tables and chairs, crowded now, were arrayed in precise alignment, the marble tabletops decorated with cheap oil-and-vinegar cruets with little earthenware *barile* in the middle, jammed full of small wooden toothpicks sharpened at both ends. Above the tables on the cream-painted walls were sad, ornate, mahogany-framed mirrors, their corners rusted where the silver backing had surrendered to years of condensation. A languid fan moved the strong-smelling smoke of cigars and

4

cigarettes lazily above the heads of the men standing alongside the zinc-topped bar on the right hand side of the café as you entered. The place had not changed for all the years Moretti had owned it. Why would one change it? To what, anyway? The twentieth century might be a lusty nine-year-old in other parts of the world, but in Sicily the times were not changing quite so fast. This was still a world of feudal castles, of peasants working the land for the aristocrats — the dukes and counts who sometimes came to the Birreria Italia to be seen, or to see. Like that old fool Giovanotti, there in the corner by the window with his bevy of fan-fluttering beauties.

There was, however, no question as to who was the centre of attention. Forty-five, perhaps, Don Vito Cascio was a man to draw the eye and hold it. Since his return to Sicily from America, he had affected a style of dress so astonishing, so different from the traditionally drab and self-effacing manner of the men of respect, that he had inspired awe. Another, ordinary, man would have been ridiculed had he dared to walk the streets of Palermo, enter the Birreria Italia, wearing the clothes of a Mississippi gambler, but Don Vito Cascio Ferro was no ordinary man. He wore the frock-coat, the dove-grey trousers, the wide-brimmed fedora hat and the pleated, ruffled shirt of white lace, with its flowing cravat, like a buccaneer. He made his own style and it looked good on him, even if it was an austere style, not a light-hearted one. Even smiling, the austerity of the man's character showed on his face. Looking at him, you knew he was a strong personality. With his hand extended to those who came to pay homage or crave a favour, he exuded a strange power, an almost tangible dignity, partly his own animal presence, but also a combination of certainty in who he was, and his place in the scheme of things. And pride. Pride in all of them.

He listened carefully to what was said by each of those who begged for the honour of speaking with him. With this one he would nod, placing a hand on the man's shoulder, lowering his head to better hear what was being said. His touch honoured the supplicant by letting others see Don Vito's friendship was a personal thing. With another, Don Vito would listen in cold and reserved silence, nodding once or twice with a look almost disdainful, his frown generating fear as easily as his smiled assent dissolved it. To have kissed his hand was to have received payment, while to have spoken warmly with him many would have ridden long baking hours on muleback from some outlying village. For Don Vito was the effective ruler of Palermo — some even said all Sicily — and all knew it. He was their rock and their refuge from the greedy Church, from the self-seeking politicians, from the money-hungry land-owners, and the indifferent storms of God. Vito Cascio Ferro, the son of a tenant farmer from Bisaquino, was their man of respect above all others.

So they came to him, one by one, and he listened to all of them, patient, benign, his attention rarely wandering. There was no question of his leaving the hot, crowded café until all who sought his aid had spoken with him. Finally, near noon, there were no more.

'*Portame un caffe*,' he said to nobody in particular. He went towards a table set in the corner of the café furthest from the door. It was covered with a clean, blue-checkered tablecloth and on it were set two small glass vases in which gay mountain flowers, picked that morning by Antonio Moretti's two children, were set. Although there was no sign to forbid it, no one ever sat at this table between the hours of ten in the morning and three in the afternoon, although it was freshly laid every day. No one, that is, except Don Vito, who relaxed into the bentwood armchair with a sigh, rocking it back slightly against the wall as was his custom, and reaching into his beautifully cut frock-coat for a *panatella*. It was lit for him, just as his coffee was brought, without his having to do more than indicate that he was ready. He sat now in the cooler rear of the café, for all the world like some Southern gentleman on the verandah of his plantation, savouring the sharp bite of the coffee and the fragrant tobacco.

Sometimes he liked to close his eyes and imagine he was again in New Orleans, the soft sweet damp warmth of the Mississippi Delta air on his face and the urgent pulse of its magic in his ears, walking down Canal Street where the field hands brought the wagons loaded with cotton bales right on into town and down to the levee. Ah, how he had loved the riverboats with their tall thin chimneys and their fretted white woodwork! They said the field hands working in the plantations upriver could tell which boat was coming from the sound of its steam-whistle: *Katie Robbins*, maybe, or the *Stack-o-Lee*, cotton-bales piled high all around her from gunwales to catwalks; seven bales high, he remembered counting, two bales deep, and maybe forty along the whole forward-to-midships section.

He shook his head slightly, as though to clear away the self-indulgent thoughts, returning reluctantly to Palermo, and to harsh, hot pink stucco, glaring in the sunlight outside the café. His *consigliere*,

Antonio Passananti, stood at his shoulder, waiting to speak. Don Vito nodded, catching sight now of the youngster, no more than twenty, who stood behind Passananti, worn peaked cap clutched in nervous hands, eyes anxiously shuttling form the face of Passananti to that of Don Vito Cascio Ferro. A Neapolitan, Don Vito thought: he has that look.

'This friend brings word from Napoli you should hear,' Antonio said softly.

'Attend me,' Don Vito said, to the young man from Naples.

'Enzo Guardasole at your command, your honour,' the youngster said. 'My father sends you his warmest affection.'

'Don Antonio is well?'

'Thank you, yes,' Enzo Guardasole said.

'This young man has come a long way, Antonio,' Don Vito said reprovingly to his *consigliore*. 'We are lacking in our duty to him. Will you take a glass of something, Enzo?'

'Thank you, Don Vitone, but no, nothing.'

'Very well,' the older man nodded.

'What is your news? Ah — quietly, though.' With no more than the movement of a finger upright across the space in front of his mouth, Don Vito stopped the boy from blurting out what he had to say. Enzo nodded, his head hanging with shame for a moment, and then began to speak so softly that even Passananti could not clearly hear what he was telling Don Vito. Passananti watched Don Vito closely: although the patrician face rarely gave away anything, he had learned over the years to watch for certain signs, like the drawing down of the right side of the bearded mouth which indicated his Don's deepest displeasure. It was the only evidence Passananti had that Don Vito even felt anger as other men.

He saw that turned-down lip now and knew Don Vito was displeased by what he had heard. He watched Don Vito nod, then nod again.

Enzo Guardasole waited, turning his peaked cap around and around in his workworn hands as the old man sat staring at him with eyes that saw nothing. For what seemed like very many minutes the tableau remained like this, frozen; and then the light came back into Don Vito's eyes and he smiled, getting languidly to his feet. He patted the young Neapolitan's back, placing a beautifully manicured hand on the coarse jacket, drawing the boy to him, hugging him affectionately.

'To have come so far in the cause of my safety is true friendship.' he said softly. 'I am in your father's debt, as I am in yours.'

Enzo Guardasole's eyes shone with pride. One of the most powerful men in Italy had openly said to him words for which princes would have gladly walked through fire. It was an enormous honour.

'Such small pleasures as my home can offer during your stay here are yours to ask for,' Don Vito added. 'My people will take care of you.' He nodded to one of the men standing by the bar and the watching man, neatly dressed in a dark blue suit, came across and stood next to Enzo Guardasole. It was understood: the boy could have anything he wanted. Anything.

Don Vito moved without haste through the crowd of people and out of the café. He acknowledged the greetings called out to him, and the hands waving to catch his attention, with an all-encompassing smile which seemed to touch each face individually but in fact never settled on any one long enough to commit him to stopping. He raised a languid hand once or twice, and then he was out in the flat noon sunshine of the street. Antonio Passananti was at his shoulder, as always. The younger man's eyes were never still, nor his body ever quite relaxed. It was not tension, but a wariness, as if he was ready for some event which, although inconceivable, might conceivably happen.

'Petrosino,' Don Vito said aloud, shaking his head as though amused slightly, surprised slightly, angry slightly.

Passananti turned at the way Don Vito said the word, frowning. He was rather a good-looking man, Passananti, thirty-seven years of age, stocky, like most Sicilians, but a little taller than the average. He was the husband of the

13

daughter of Don Vitone's brother, but also more than that. As Don Vito's *consigliere*, he was lieutenant, executive officer, adviser, counsellor, sounding-board, manager of the many enterprises in which Don Vito Cascio Ferro had an interest. His power was almost as the power of Don Vitone, for he spoke for the Don. He had never abused his power and he would never need to. Passananti was the ideal lieutenant: he had no ambition. He did not smoke, he did not drink, he gambled only rarely. He loved his wife and she provided him with all the sexual adventure he would ever need. If there were those who said he had machine oil in his veins instead of blood, well, they never said it to his face.

'Petrosino?' he echoed.

'A policeman,' Don Vito said. 'From America. The boy brought word he is in Naples. That he has been in Rome. Asking questions.'

'A policeman,' Passananti mused. 'Is he very important?' He used the word in the Sicilian way, meaning does he merit one's respect?

14

'Important?' mused Don Vito. 'Perhaps. I don't know. But brave, certainly. A good soldier. Not too much brain, but stupidly courageous and for that reason not to be underestimated. Here,' he said, handing Passananti a piece of paper. 'Read this.'

It was a newspaper cutting and Passananti raised an eyebrow in an unspoken question.

'The *Herald* of New York,' Don Vito supplied. 'Of 20 February, 1909.'

Passananti nodded and started reading. ''As the first act of the new Secret Service he has founded, Commissioner Binghan has authorized Lieutenant Joseph Petrosino to travel to Italy, and in particular to Sicily, where he is to assemble important information concerning those Italian criminals resident in the United States, and in particular in New York City, whom the police, in order to proceed for their deportation, need to provide documentary evidence against — evidence only obtainable in Italy.' '

He looked at Don Vito. 'Are they mad?' he asked.

'Perhaps,' Don Vito said. 'Foolhardy might be a better word.'

Passananti read the rest of the article, which confirmed that when the evidence which Petrosino was going to collect was assembled, it would be possible to bring prosecutions against many known criminals who had heretofore been able to evade the law.

'This Petrosino,' Passananti asked. 'Do you know him?'

'No, I've never seen him. But I know much about him. As I think he may know about me.'

'You think he is coming to Palermo.' It wasn't a question.

'He is. The boy said so.'

'And it angers you.' Again, not a question.

'No,' said Don Vito reflectively. 'It doesn't anger me. Let us say I find it unacceptable.'

He gestured towards the street. 'Come, walk with me down to the harbour and I'll tell you the story,' he said. 'Then later we'll discuss what must be done with Petrosino.'

'You want him killed?'

'Perhaps,' Don Vito said. 'I haven't decided yet.'

He might have been talking about the weather.

2

'Of course,' Don Vito said, 'you understand no story ever truly begins or ends. There is a point at which one enters it, and another at which one leaves it. But the story itself never ends.

'I understand,' Passananti said.

'Then we shall begin in Bisaquino, thirty years or so ago,' Don Vito said.

★　★　★

Bisaquino, bleached by a sun as relentless as the conquerors who had marched beneath it through the centuries. Bisaquino, covered by an ochre dust that sifts, moves, constant and inescapable, gritting between the teeth when you eat, staining the wilting washing hanging on string between the houses. Weeds and drooping hollyhocks grow in the dark dirt where angles of the walls provide enough shade for them to sow their own seeds.

Garbage piles high in the central gutters on the side alleys, waiting for a rain that rarely comes to wash it away. Flies buzz.

Bisaquino, one long street, stone-stepped, carved from the rocky land itself, where children play squalling games among roaming pigs and goats and chickens outside the one-room houses, *bassi*, Neapolitan style, the whole family living in them. The long stepped street drops down and on down again until it ends abruptly, nowhere, petering out in the open, hostile terrain. The land lies before the eyes, empty, dun, bare; no hedges, no trees, no walls, no houses. It rolls away inimically towards the mountains, their sides scarred and gullied like the faces of the old men, and beyond them the higher mountains lying slate blue against the bone-yellow sky. Above them falcons soar, high-pitched squeals coming from them like the laments of frustrated phantoms searching for life in the prehistoric landscape below them. But it is empty, nothing moves. And it is silent.

Gabriele Pantucci remembered the silence most.

After all these years in America, you would think an old man might forget the days of his boyhood, but he remembered Bisaquino as vividly as if he had clumped down the stone-staired street only an hour ago. At fourteen he could stand it no more, and like all his cousins, all his friends — no, he corrected himself, most of his friends — he had made the long journey to America. Away at last from the stinking *strega* with their potions and amulets; away from the priests who castigated women who did not bear a child each year for denying souls to God; away from the backbreaking day labour that had started when he was nine; away from the plaster saints and the monotony of *pasta* without meat and the smell of goats forever on your clothing.

He came to America long before the millions who would follow, long before the *padrones* learned to wait for their unsuspecting countrymen at the foot of the ferry slip on Cortlandt Street and sign them into bondage, long before the area around Mulberry Street became known as 'Little Italy.'

He was taken care of, he had friends. His own *paisan*, Accursio Ferro, who was a *campiere* on the farm of Santa Maria del Bosco in Bisaquino, who managed the place for the English *barone* who owned it, had seen to it that Gabriele, the godfather of Accursio's first son Vito, had a bed to go to, a home to live in, a job of work to do. It was not a question of payment, or honour, or debt. It was a thing that Don Accursio did for those who came to him and asked help. A favour, a helping hand; nothing more. Your thanks, your friendship, were his reward.

Gabriele worked in a grocery store on Broome Street which was owned by an Italian family, from Milano, and they were kind to him. They taught him manners, smoothed out the harshness of his Sicilian vowels, made sure he went to school to learn how to write and read English, saw to it that he became a citizen.

He married their daughter, Catarina,

and, when the old man died a few years later, he took over the running of the store. He watched as the trickle of Italian immigrants turned into a river, a spate, a flood; always ready to help newcomers, to listen to their problems, find them some sort of solution to whatever problem they could not themselves solve. As his patronage grew, so did his business. He became an importer of olive oil, fine cheeses, hams from Parma, the food without which the immigrants refused to live. They brought Italy with them; they remained always Italian. They were like children in many ways, and Don Gabriele, as they now called him, watched over them as if they were, for the good Lord had seen fit not to bless him with any of his own.

He learned, too, how to manage the other elements which threatened his own success and the safety of his own people: the vicious thugs who were members of the cutthroat street gangs — the Five Pointers and the Hudson Dusters, the Monk Eastman mob and the Gashouse gang — as well as the bombthrowers, the

22

anarchisti, the *Camorristi* who brought their Neapolitan tricks of extortion and murder to the streets of Little Italy, the *banditti* of the Black Hand, and other *mafiosi* who came in the swelling horde of immigrants which arrived on the shores of America in the 1880s. Don Gabriele reasoned with them, counselled them, and occasionally, when it was necessary, used the power which he now had to chasten them. He tried to teach them without pain what it had taken him decades to learn: that in New York the Irish controlled the politics, the Jews the banking, just as they did in most other large cities, and that they, the Italians, must take care in attempting to get some share — he used the mafia phrase *fari vagnari a pizzu*, to dip the beak — of whatever there was to get a share of.

With his habitual courtesy and talent for understatement, Don Gabriele had to some degree united the warring factions, but diplomacy did not always work on these young men fresh from the old country, who saw how it was in the new place and wished only to get their hands upon as much money as they could, as quickly as they could. So, despite his dissuasions, they went to prison with monotonous regularity for stupid things, things like counterfeiting, selling the bodies of women, physical violence outside their own territories; things he would have counselled against. They never realized that to attract the attention of the police in New York was one thing: it could be bought off, or a favour from someone at Tammany could be asked in return for another given. But the Federal authorities, no: they were generally efficient and normally incorruptible. It was foolish to draw them into one's orbit.

But Don Gabriele was old now, and tired. He had not achieved his lifetime dream, to bring together all the disparate and warring factions of his own city and all the other cities which had their Little Italies: Pittsburgh and New Orleans and Chicago and Philadelphia; to form a confederation, a state within the United States, to which all Italians might turn in trouble. He shook his head, fondling the ears of the old dog which grunted in its sleep at the side of his chair.

Still they would not learn, he thought sadly. Maranzano now in Brooklyn, massing his *Camorristi* to show strength against Morello and Lupo here in Manhattan. If they were not controlled, they would go to war like the Provenanzos and the Matrangas had done in New Orleans a dozen years before, fighting like dogs in the street over the right to control the waterfront. Not content with exposing themselves to full public attention, they had killed the police chief who had declared himself dedicated to stamping out the gang warfare. To use the *lupara*, the heavy shotgun so closely identified with our thing, on the streets of an American city in the year 1890, *Dio, Dio*, the mind refused to believe!

There had been terrible anti-Italian riots; vigilante gangs swarming through the streets dragged the men who had been arrested for the murder out of the jail and hung them to the lamp-posts. What it had cost in lawyers, endless battalions of lawyers! And then the job of restoring the face, expunging the consciousness of the thing from the mind of the public, returning to anonymity. He did not want that again, and especially not here in New York. What happened in New Orleans had remained local, more or less. If the same sort of thing started to happen in New York, it would become international news.

So he had journeyed back to the old country, and taken counsel. There he had met the son of his old friend Accursio, his own godson Vito Cascio Ferro who had taken his father's place and strengthened the respect his father had commanded into an almost astonishing power. Don Gabriele had known, immediately he saw the way young Vito walked into a room, that this was the man he wanted to bring to America. This was the man who could unite the warring factions, the man who might even realize the dream Don Gabriele knew he could no longer effect alone. This was a man to whom all of the others would listen without question, counsel with, bow to.

He spoke with Vito Cascio Ferro, his godson, and he spoke with the council. It was agreed. And on the first of August, 1902, Vito embarked at Marsiglia for the voyage to the United States.

3

There were many changes to make.

To begin with, almost as if he felt he could let go now, secure in the knowledge that what he had begun would be continued, old Don Gabriele died. Peacefully, in his sleep, the nightcap tilted forward over his strangely unlined face, during the night of Wednesday, 22 April, 1903. Almost as if he had not wanted to be a nuisance: Easter well past, and midweek, so there was plenty of time to arrange for funeral ceremonies and visits from those who would wish to pay respect to his mortal remains at a week-end rather than any other time. His lying-in-state, for such it virtually was, in the small house on Charlton Street, jammed the streets of Little Italy as effectively shut as if the New York Police Department had erected barricades. From all over the area ordinary people trekked across town carrying small bunches of spring flowers, small gifts of respect; old men and women, young children, all waited patiently beside the railings until their turn came to go inside the house, along the hall and to the left into the parlour where the old man lay, rigid in his satin-lined mahogany coffin, dressed in the fine blue suit he had hardly ever worn, the old patrician nose as hawklike in death as ever it had been in life.

Mingling with the ordinary people came some others: better-dressed usually, more prosperous-looking, jewellery sometimes catching light from the watery spring sunshine. From Brooklyn they came, and from the Bronx, and over in New Jersey. From Cleveland and Buffalo silent representatives, sweating in heavy wool suits, paid their respects. From Chicago's south side came others, and from New Orleans. These found hotel rooms nearby in the Tenderloin, knowing there was much to be discussed in the wake of the old Don's death.

The house and the tiny garden in front of it, the railings, steps and hallways, were buried beneath ornate and lavish floral wreaths whose perfume sweetened the dusty tang of the street. Don Vito sent out chilled wine and little biscuits to the people waiting to file past Don Gabriele's body. Passengers aboard the horse-trams clattering by on their way down to the Chambers Street ferry turned their heads as they went by, surprised and intrigued by the size of the crowds around the unspectacular little house. A couple of patrolmen kept a weather eye on the crush, but there was never so much as a hint of trouble. As if anyone in the entire Italian community would have made so much as an impolite noise outside the home of the deceased Don Gabriele on this day of all days!

And so the ritual was performed and the rules were observed, and by the Sunday night the coffin had departed for the docks on the first stage of its journey back to Palermo, where Don Gabriele had decided he wanted finally to be buried. That same Sunday night, Vito Cascio Ferro held his first council with the representatives of all the families who had come to Manhattan, all the representatives of those who already lived in Manhattan. There was wine, plenty of it, chilled in a wooden crate standing over a block of ice in the stone-floored kitchen. They sat in the room where the coffin had been.

'It is time for change,' Don Vito told them. 'Time for considering new ways of co-operating instead of warring among ourselves.'

Some of those in the room looked at each other knowingly: yes, their looks seemed to say, and the man who can get the Castellamarese to work with the Neapolitans, and then get either or both to co-operate with anyone else, is going to pull quite a trick. Not that their private thoughts indicated any disrespect for their host; far from it. They respected Don Vito highly, as they had Don Gabriele before him. They knew that what he was saying to them now was by way of suggestion, a proposition he would like them to take back for discussion among their own families. The least they could do was listen to him, hear him out.

So they listened, and as he talked their

polite scepticism slowly melted. They began to lean forward in their seats. Their eyes began to show animation for the very first time since they had all assembled.

Vito Cascio Ferro told them a parable.

It was about a stupid farmer who owned a cow. The winter got very bad and he had no food, so he killed the cow and ate its meat. He lived well that one winter, but the next winter he starved to death. Now if he'd had the sense to realize that he could milk the cow forever, use the milk to barter for anything else he wanted, feed his children from the milk, and still own the cow, he might have been a richer man. And so it was with this thing of ours, he told them.

'We can live off the milk, and forever off the milk of the offspring of the original cow, but we must change ourselves to do it, just like that farmer. There must be an end to this internecine warfare, where each family goes to the mattresses because of some stupid infringement of territory.'

'Such things,' said Lupo of the East Side, 'are not so stupid.'

'Not stupid, I agree,' Don Vito said, 'but without arbitration all fighting is stupid, for who can call a halt to it? I propose that there will be a central council to adjudicate in such matters. It will decide what is best for all of us, not just for any one of us. It will enforce those decisions if it has to, with the power of all those who sit upon it.'

'And how does Don Vito propose that such a council be formed?' grunted Pelligrino Morano, who controlled the Brooklyn territory.

A new system, Don Vito explained. A chain of command, each level of authority linked with the next and the next only; the one beyond that knowing nothing of the one below-but-one or above-but-one. The old rules would remain roughly the same, of course. Each band, or *regime* had always elected its own *capo*, always would. Except that Don Vito now proposed that the internal *regime* could in turn hire mercenaries from anywhere they chose: Torrio's street gangs in the Five Points for example; or wherever they could. These soldiers, *soldati*, would be just that: not required to think, to swear the oath. They would be disposable manpower and they would be able to point the finger at no one except one member of the *regime* from whom they would have had orders.

'There will be a new rank,' he told them, 'which I propose shall be called *caporegime*. This man will run the teams who run the soldiers. He reports, of course, as do all the *caporegime* in the organization, to the *consigliere* or the *capofamiglia*, or both. It will provide a safety factor, a means of preventing betrayal and treachery, which I am sure,' he said, permitting himself a sly grin, 'you will agree is to be desired.'

'This council of which you spoke, the squat Calvocoressi from Buffalo asked, 'who will sit in that?'

'Each head of family,' Don Vito said, 'and his counsellor.'

'And who will be the head of the council?' the thickset Calvocoressi insisted. 'You?'

'We first must see,' Don Vito said gently, 'if everyone agrees that such a council is the best way for our thing. Then that council must agree upon a time and place to meet. At that time and place its first duty will be to choose a leader. After that has been done, Don Pietro, I may be able to reply.'

There were some thin smiles: Don Vito wasn't falling for anything as obvious as that.

'There are other things more important for our discussion,' Don Vito said, 'than who will head the council. Working together, for instance. On things which benefit all of us, not just the local people. We must remember those things Don Gabriele has already taught us and which we still forget: that the Irish control the politics and the Jews most of the finance, and it will take many, many years until we can change that. Meantime there are rich areas awaiting exploration and I name but a few which come swiftly to my mind: the docks, the markets, the railways, the inter-city transportation companies. The distribution of ice during the summer. All of them areas which do not attract a great deal of police attention and even less attention from the Federal authorities. Let us concentrate upon them, systematize them. Together,' he said in closing, 'we can do it.'

There were many questions.

He listened to them all carefully, answering fully, holding nothing back. Sometimes he let them talk it out among themselves, leaning back in the protesting wicker chair that had been Don Gabriele's favourite, sipping his Capri wine, his hooded eyes watching each man for a moment, weighing, assessing, judging him. Then on to the next. Sometimes he would interrupt, to reinforce a valid point someone else had made. But there was not a great deal of discussion. There didn't need to be, and all of them knew it. The real answers to the propositions which Don Vito had put forward would come from the men who made the decisions for their families all over the country.

When the business was done with, they talked as friends for a while about mutual interests, families, people coming from the Old Country and those going back to it. They talked about some of their own businesses: what they found was going well, what not so well. They were like any other group of businessmen meeting, perhaps on the occasion of the death of their company's President, branch managers talking shop, speculating upon the succession. Except that they were *mafiosi* to a man, and their business was blackmail, extortion, and murder; their talk of scaled punishments for transgressors against the laws of *omerta*, rewards and promotions for effective beatings and killings.

One by one, late that Sunday night, the visitors left the house. No promises were given, no blood oaths sworn. Each man respected the other; all respected Don Vito Cascio Ferro. There was no need to put that respect into words: the rough *abbraccio* indicated that Don Vito's request — for he had asked no favour — that his thoughts be considered carefully would be carried whence they had come. And the answers would come back, yes or no, with a similar respect implicit and expected.

Finally only Ignazo Lupo and his *consigliere*, Nicholas Morello, remained in the room with Don Vito and Antonio Lombrado. Lombrado had been *consigliere* to Don Gabriele, as he now was to Don Vito. He was an old man now, his face lined with the wounds of the years, the wisdom of a fox who has been in every trap devised by man behind his hooded old eyes. Ignazo Lupo was thin-faced, hollow-cheeked. His hair was lank and greasy, and beneath heavy black brows his olive-black eyes were deepset and shadowed. He was squat and heavily built, and almost seventy years of age. He used an Anglicized version of his own surname over on the East Side: Lupo the Wolf, they called him there. Don Vito had snorted when he had first been told this nonsense and he was no more impressed with Lupo now than he had been the first time they had met.

Lupo's *consigliere*, Nicholas Morello, however, was something else again. Much taller than the bulky Lupo, slimly built and elegantly dressed, almost to the point of dandyism, Morello was young and intelligent and ambitious. He had let all this be known without ever so much as speaking a word of praise for himself, and had Don Vito's attention, not admiration, because of it.

Delicately now, and diplomatically, Lupo and his counsellor talked of the reason behind their request for a private talk with Don Vito. Their desire to discuss a certain, well, he wouldn't say problem, not to call it something it wasn't, but a difficulty, yes, certainly that, Lupo said.

'You know, of course,' Lupo said, 'that the Irish hate all Italians. And especially Sicilians.'

Don Vito said nothing: next they would tell him that three came after two, he thought. However, he waited.

'Still, we do business with them. They are useful,' Lupo went on. 'When they come to us, or to some of our people, with their stolen paper, we broker it for them. Ten per cent of the face value: you know how it works.

'My God,' Don Vito thought, 'will he explain that to me now?'

Everyone knew how the stolen paper

racket worked. The street gangs — most of them Irish, some of them Jewish — ruled the alleys and sidewalks of Manhattan. From the upper West Side, the area they were calling Hell's Kitchen these days, down through Chelsea and into the Village, the scabrous, peeling rows of tenements bred new reinforcements for the gangs of street fighters who banded together, dubbing themselves defiantly with fighting-cock names, and terrorized their 'patches'. It was well known that Richard Croker, who had run the graft-ridden Tammany machine created by his predecessor, 'Boss' Tweed, and still remained a power in city politics, had begun his career as leader of the Fourth Avenue Tunnel Gang, making his living then, as did the gangs today, by extortion, terrorism and theft.

One of the more common of their crimes was to steal negotiable stocks or bonds — a caper originally perfected by Dutch Heinrich up in Hell's Kitchen back in the seventies — either by walking into a brokerage house and snatching them, or by stealing them under cover of a well studied diversion, or by pretending to be a messenger: there were half a hundred ways. They were all the same to the Whyoes and the Gophers and the Dusters and the Hell's Kitchen mob. Disposing of the paper once stolen was another thing again, and usually beyond the ability of the street thugs. So they brought them down to the Bowery or the Five Points, who in turn passed them on to the Italians. They'd learned not to go to the Jews long since; and the Italians, even if you didn't like them, never argued. It was ten per cent on the barrel and no questions asked.

The bonds or stocks, or whatever it was, were used to float bank loans by using them as security, the whole deal fronted by some nominee of the *amici*. He would collect the loan, hand it over, receive his payment, and disappear back into the warrens of Little Italy. In due course the loan would fall due, be defaulted, and the bank would attempt to get its money back by cashing the paper, only to discover, too late, that the paper was worthless, the serial numbers having been cancelled immediately subsequent to the theft. It was a relatively easy and painless way to finance other activities, and most of the families used it in one form or another. Lupo the Wolf had come up with a new twist on the formula: he paid off the thieves who brought him the paper with counterfeit money.

He saw the faint hint of a frown on Don Vito's face as he revealed this, hastening to add that he had ventured into counterfeiting only because of a temporary lack of capital at a time of expansion: some real estate in Coney Island for which he had needed funds. As soon as the deal was completed, naturally, he had intended to abandon the project. In fact, it was about this very matter that he wished to ask Don Vito's advice, for there were other matters connected with it.

Don Vito Cascio Ferro nodded and said nothing, but he was thinking thoughts that would have turned Lupo the Wolf's bowels to jelly had he been able to read them.

In fact, he had been expecting this plea

for help from Lupo and he knew why it was being made. He had his own sources of intelligence in the *quartiere* and he despised Lupo for not having the common sense to realize it and to accord him at least a frankness concomitant with that fact. He did not mind being treated like a fool — it gave him an enormous advantage — but it irritated him when it was unnecessary. He knew, for instance (and knew that Lupo knew), that a special investigator from the Department of Justice in Washington had been poking around asking questions fairly close to the tracks Lupo and his associates had left. The investigator's name was Flynn, and even though he had been as easy to watch as a hippopotamus in an aviary, he had still managed to break up the Pittsburgh operation, sending it in disarray to Manhattan, where Lupo had sheltered it. The man Flynn had sent one of the counterfeiters to Sing Sing for a three-to-five, and was still on Lupo's tail, which explained some of Lupo's nervousness. The rest of it could be explained by the fact that the leader of the counterfeiters was Benedetto Madonnia, one of Lupo's own family, who was said to be gathering support for a challenge to Lupo's leadership. If Lupo decreed that the counterfeiting must cease, then Madonnia might make his challenge.

All this Don Vito knew, all of it he had discussed at length with his own counsellor, Lombrado. Lombrado knew them all much better than he, Vito, did, and his advice was sage, measured.

'If I were Lupo,' Lombrado had said, 'I would fear a disgruntled counterfeiter far less than he seems to do, and spend more time wondering why my *consigliere* had not already taken steps to solve my problem.'

Don Vito had been startled by this inference. No *consigliere* had ever betrayed his *capo*, not in all the history of the *amici*. It was infamous to suggest it, and if it were remotely near true, then it was his duty to Lupo to advise him of that fact. Lombrado had held up a hand in gentle remonstration. Wait, he had advised. Wait and see: the wisdom of the ages in three words. Don Vito had smiled. And agreed.

So he listened now to Lupo, and saw the justice of Lombrado's advice. Lupo was old, and frightened. It showed in his bearing, quivered in his voice as he asked for help, for direction, for support. It was very difficult for Lupo to put into words the fact that he might not be able to control one of his own family. He was trying to find a way of saying it. Don Vito led him gently to that point.

'What would be the total sum involved in this enterprise, this false money? How much per year?' he asked.

'Hard to say,' Lupo shrugged. 'Five hundred thousand, maybe.'

'For so little, you risk so much?' Don Vito allowed himself to sound astonished. 'When you can make ten times as much my way — without the risk of prison? He shook his head in sorrowing astonishment.

'You are right,' Lupo said, humbly. 'As always, Don Vitone. It shall cease.'

'Except — ' Morello said, softly, prompting.

'Yes, yes, except,' Lupo said. He didn't

want to put it into words but he knew he had to now. They were all waiting. No one was going to do any more for him. 'Except. Except there may be dissension inside my family.' He rushed the words out and then looked fearfully from beneath his brows at Don Vito, not knowing what to expect.

Whatever it was, Don Vito did not oblige him: he merely nodded, absently, as if his mind was elsewhere. 'That is a problem, indeed,' Don Vito said. 'And I must give it some thought. Meanwhile, go home. Go about your business. Leave your worries here for a while.'

He permitted Lupo to kiss his hand, keeping his face austere as he received the *abbraccio*, bidding Lupo and his *consigliere* safety and Godspeed as they left the little house. His face was expressionless as Lombrado poured him the last glass of the Capri wine.

'Well?' he said at last. It was only just a question.

'Lupo?' Lombrado said. 'An old-style street gangster, I suppose. He's not up to date, but he's still effective enough.'

46

Don Vito nodded. He admired Lombrado's oblique way of speaking his thoughts: perfectly clear and decided, yet always containing just enough deference, just enough awareness of the lieutenant's place.

'This Madonnia,' Don Vito said.

'I'll put it in hand,' Lombrado replied.

That was another thing he liked about Lombrado: he seemed to pick up the thought almost as you formed it. Quite a remarkable man. No wonder Don Gabriele had placed such implicit trust in him, had insisted Vito accept no other as his counsellor.

'Where is he from, by the way?' Don Vito asked.

'Madonnia? His people are from Tuscany, I think.'

'Ah,' Don Vito said, as if that explained everything.

★   ★   ★

The Stella d'Italia was over on Elizabeth Street. It was a pleasant walk from the house in Charlton Street, a dozen blocks

47

east, across Sixth and along Prince Street, past St Patrick's on the corner of Mott. If there was a special exhibition at Niblo's Garden, Don Vito could look in, wander around for ten minutes before continuing across town to his destination. The restaurant was only a small place, with perhaps a dozen tables in all, set out like any southern Italian *trattoria* with checkered tablecloths and wine bottles with candles stuck in them, electroplated knives, forks, and spoons, already laid at each place, with a big rough cotton napkin of matching check between them. Along the right-hand wall were four big booths, eight places to each table: family tables for those who came in on Sunday for Teresa Fontana's good plain cooking.

Don Gabriele had taken at least two meals here every week for most of his life. He had introduced Vito Cascio Ferro to Teresa and her husband, Franco, in such a way that it was ensured that whenever Vito asked for a table one would become available immediately, with no other closer than six feet. Don Vito had later intimated that he preferred to sit in a corner of the room, away from windows, and it had been so arranged: a round table in the back of the room, at which, when Don Vito arrived with Lombrado, Lupo the Wolf and another man were already sitting, chewing on pieces of bread, and sipping the good wine they had received automatically as guests of Don Vito. The Fontana family looked upon this service as an investment, a kind of insurance. Certainly, in all these years, they had never had a broken window, much less a visit from some of the roughnecks who were always trying to muscle themselves a few bucks out of protection rackets. Franco Fontana would shrug fatalistically when his wife scolded him with the cost of one of Don Vito's bigger parties. What the devil! he would say. If he didn't take it this way, the *amici* would take it some other way.

Benedetto Madonnia was a chunky, solidly built man who, when he stood to greet Don Vito, revealed he stood perhaps six feet two inches tall. His skin was freckled, and his hair a sandy blond, thin on top and receding deeply above the temples, cut very close to the scalp and brushed straight back. Two heavy lines spread from his wide-flared nose to the corners of a mouth that closed like a trap as soon as he let the smile slide off his face. He wore a dark blue suit with a casual shirt open at the neck. Coarse wiry hair sprouted at the base of his throat. His hands were thick-fingered and powerful. He emanated physical strength, animal power, and even if he was impressed to be in the company of this man of respect, Don Vito Cascio Ferro, there was a light in his eyes that said he was determined not to let it show; a defiant look on the pale killer's face that Don Vito could hardly have avoided noticing.

'Try the *zuppa di cozze*,' Don Vito said. 'It's very fine.'

Ignazo Lupo and Lombrado nodded, but Madonnia said no, he'd rather have something light. '*Ho avutto troppo di vitto recentemente*,' he said. Literally translated, that meant he'd been eating too much lately, but no one at the table was misled for a moment. The direct pun on their host's name was very obvious, and very clumsy: therefore deliberate. 'I've been getting too much Vito lately' was what Madonnia had said.

Lupo the Wolf's cheek twitched visibly when he heard the words, as though someone had jammed a hatpin into his thigh. Lombrado had his head down and he managed to keep it that way, while Don Vito himself, if he heard the word-play, gave no sign at all in anything he did. He played the perfect host, getting Madonnia to talk about himself, emptying the wine bottle and calling for more when Zia Teresa brought the steaming pasta, cooked *al dente* the way Don Vito liked it. Madonnia told him that he was thirty-three, that he had come to America when he was seven, that in many ways he considered himself more of an American now than an Italian. All through the meal the older man nodded with great interest, asking the occasional question which drew Madonnia out even further, and increased the contempt Madonnia felt for this stupid old Sicilian peasant who made noises when he drank his soup. He was a big man and it took a lot of wine to get to him; but Don Vito was making sure that there *was* a lot of wine, and that it was getting to Madonnia, who grew louder as it did. He talked on about the ways of making money he'd thought of which nobody else had even considered yet — such was his vanity, thought Lombrado, watching Don Vito now all the time, hardly hearing Madonnia's braggadocio — and all the time he did, his distaste and loathing grew.

Didn't these backward old despots know that time was running out on them? The newer generation, the ones born in America, weren't going to sit around letting a thousand rackets go to waste because some bunch of fucking illiterate Sicilian peasants was running things. God! look at him, he thought, swigging his wine. Still full of all the superstitions he learned at the tits of the *strega*, sticking to the rules they learned in the old country because they hadn't either the imagination or the guts to create new ones here. They just plain couldn't adapt, alter, change things. Stupid old goats! Half of them never even learned a word of the language of their new country, couldn't even take a streetcar away out of Little Italy because they'd get lost, being unable to read the street signs on the one hand, and congenitally unable to ask directions (or anything else) from a cop on the other. The teeming streets were full of angles they didn't know how to exploit: policing the numbers, the shy-locking, the protection rackets, the bail-bondsmen, paying off the cops, fixing the ward-heelers, and a thousand more. They knew nothing; not a damned thing. Moustache Petes, some of the younger ones (when alone together) called them.

And this one, this Don Vito, he was a prototype, a real ginger peach. Look at him: baggy old jacket, flannel pants, street shoes that had seen considerably better days, a flannel shirt with no collar. He looked like he'd just got off the boat. Dammit! if a man was in the money, he ought to look it. It gave him a certain standing on the streets. People knew you were somebody, stood back a little, gave you air. Who'd give this stupid old goat the time of day?

Perhaps some of it showed in his voice when he spoke, or perhaps Don Vito had expected nothing else. After all, he was armed with the information about Madonnia which Lombrado had brought to him. It was a very thorough dossier indeed, and left little about Madonnia's life to Don Vito's imagination.

He found it hard to believe that a man could be as *lentezza*, as backward, as lacking in intelligence, as this man seemed to be. The fact that he *was* in turn told Don Vito something about Ignazo Lupo; but for the moment he filed that thought away in his formidable memory. Madonnia, he saw, was a big man, with appetites to match. His speech was as coarse as his methods were reported to be. He was well known, according to Lombrado, in every brothel south of Fourteenth Street, and behind his back as a *pezzonovanta*, a 'big shot' with more mouth than money. Madonnia spent lavishly, but mostly on himself: he drank Scotch whisky neat, nothing else, and when drunk — which was often — became loudmouthed and belligerent.

There were several stories of fights in the street which had all but ended in his killing men. And, of course, he *had* killed; but not yet outside the line of his own duties, Lombrado's report said.

Madonnia also supported a shyster lawyer who, apparently, ran a fairly successful pimping racket on the side. The lawyer was to fix any cops who might get the urge to smack Madonnia over the head with a nightstick and slap him in the Tombs; or to get across town to one of the judges known to the *amici* who would sell you a writ of habeas corpus as readily as any pushcart pedlar would sell you an apple. A slightly higher price, of course; say a grand per each, five if you really wanted the hurry-up treatment and the charge was murder, one or two.

Don Vito had shaken his head in quiet surprise that a man with a responsibility not only to the *amici* but to his own family, his colleagues, should let trivialities like liquor and prostitutes affect his judgment (and what of his tongue?) to the extent that he was known to every patrolman north of the 'deadline' as a guinea troublemaker who was gonna wind up bent double in a PD-basket one of these days, the kind that got every Italian smeared with the epithet 'dago'.

Of course none of this showed in so much as one shift of one plane of Don Vito's face. He was ever the polite host, even when, at last, he brought the conversation round to the counterfeiting. He mentioned, offhandedly, his own feeling that it would probably be better for the whole organization, bearing in mind the interest of the Federal investigators, if these activities — however nominally profitable — were for the moment discontinued.

'But that's just plain damned stupid!' Madonnia said loudly, much too far gone with the wine to notice the paleness of Don Vito's face as he swallowed the insult. 'Stupid, stupid! You know what that business could be worth?'

'Whatever it is worth,' Vito said, 'it is not worth attracting the attention of Federal investigators. It is not worth getting our people put into prison. There are other, more profitable areas we — '

' — to your other areas!' Madonnia snapped, making the sign with the thumbnail beneath the front teeth which is the Italian's final insult to anything, 'and — to your Feds, too! I can handle them.'

'Agreed,' Don Vito said, imperturbable while Lupo and Lombrado quailed. 'They are not formidable, but they are patient. They have all the time in the world on their side. It is of no import to them whether our people go to jail for seven years today or tomorrow. Only that finally they go. It is this I wish to avoid.'

'Like to see 'em try nailing any of my people, thassall,' Madonnia said.

'But they have already,' Don Vito pointed out. 'Di Primo, was he not arrested in Pittsburgh?'

'Ah, Di Primo,' Madonnia said. 'They're welcome to little fish like Giuseppe.'

'Our people are not divided into little fish and big fish,' Don Vito said, softly. 'They are all our people.'

'Listen, I know about that,' Madonnia said. 'But you're not listening — '

'No!' This time Don Vito's voice had an edge to it, and Madonnia stopped in the middle of his sentence. He hadn't heard this tone before, and, without knowing why, he obeyed it instantly.

'No,' Don Vito went on, in a softer voice. 'You are not listening, Benedetto. I am asking you, as a favour to me personally, to suspend these counterfeiting operations, and to concentrate upon other — '

That was as far as he got.

'Wait a goddamned minute there!' Madonnia blared, banging the flat of his hand on the table. Lombrado flinched, and Lupo turned away, his eyes full of fear. 'Just hold on a fuckin' minute!' Madonnia said. A woman in one of the booths frowned, and said something to the man alongside her.

'Benedetto, *per piacere*', Lupo pleaded, laying his hand on the big man's forearm. '*Dolcemente*, quietly, please.'

'Ah, take your crawling hands off me, you old fart!' snapped Madonnia. 'I've had it up to here with you and your Sicilian friends. This is the US of A,

Lupo, not darkest fuckin' Palermo!'

'But of course,' Don Vito said, his voice still soft, still gentle. 'It is for this reason that we counsel together, try to cooperate. We seek no fight with you, Benedetto.'

The very mildness of his voice, the admission he had made, strengthened rather then diluted Madonnia's determination to have it out with them here and now. He felt a surge of confidence flow through him: the old *capraio* was running scared.

'That's smart of you,' he allowed. 'It don't pay to mess none with me. Now you listen to what I got to say, right?' He sloshed some more red wine into his glass, staining the tablecloth with his spillage as he did.

Don Vito spread his hands in a placating gesture. 'That is why we are here, to listen.'

'Well, *paisan*,' Madonnia said, leering on the word, 'I put a lot of time and effort into settin' up this little thing of mine, *capisce*? I was the one found the engraver. I was the one put up the front money for him to come in from

Pittsburgh. I was the one brought the whole deal in, come to that. Now you tell me hard luck, Nitto, we want you to forget the whole thing. Half a million smackers a year, forget it. All the money it cost you, write it off. Well, *paisan'* — again the sneer on the word — 'no fuckin' soap. I sure as hell ain't passin' up my piece of that kind of dough. I told Lupo he was out of his head to think of it, or listen to you. Shit! how's any of us know you ain't planning to take the whole racket over yourself and pocket the proceeds?'

As he said this, Lombrado flinched visibly, as though a small stone had struck his face. He cast down his eyes. Lupo turned his head away, thick lips flat with astonishment at Madonnia's error. For anyone to suggest that Don Vito might steal was bad enough. For it to be suggested that he would steal from the *amici* was an insult so breathtaking that it defied comprehension. Even Madonnia felt the shocked silence, although in his semi-drunken state he was not altogether aware of exactly what he had just said.

Once again Vito Cascio Ferro wondered how this overgrown ape with the table manners of an animal had risen in Lupo's family, and what this told him about that family. He did not look at Lombrado, did not need to. He knew that Lombrado had made the arrangements he had been expected to make, knew that Lombrado was now only awaiting the sign that Don Vito wished to exercise his indubitable right to expunge the insults which had been thrown at him this night. Yet still Don Vito tried once more.

'I am sorry that you do not feel as we do,' he said. 'I had hoped we might reach agreement like reasonable men.'

'We already did,' Madonnia said. 'Hey, some more wine here!'

Zia Teresa waited for Don Vito's almost imperceptible nod before bringing another bottle of Bardolino. She banged it on the table, her minor protest at Madonnia's loud obscenities.

'Of course, you could buy me off,' Madonnia said slyly, pouring himself a glass of wine.

'You mean — pay you not to work

against our interests?'

'Sure,' Madonnia said, waving a sloppy arm. 'You pay off everyone else. Cops. Judges. Firemen. Safety inspectors. Health inspectors. Everyone gets paid. Why not me?'

Don Vito looked at Madonnia for a long moment, weighing the man. 'That is not our way,' he said quietly.

'Then maybe you better learn some new ways, old man,' Madonnia said.

'Perhaps,' Don Vito agreed. 'Perhaps you are right.'

'Bet your fuckin' ass I am!' Madonnia said, lurching to his feet. 'You *paisans* think about it, okay? Think it over, what I told you. You want to contact me, you know where to find me.' He started away from the table, and then almost as an afterthought lurched back, putting his meaty hands flat on the table and thrusting his face towards Don Vito's. 'And none of your fuckin' Sicilian games, *paisan*!' he rumbled. 'Anything happens to me — anything unexpected, like — and someone at Police Headquarters gets a long letter.'

'Ah,' Don Vito said softly. 'A letter.'

Madonnia had certainly done it all, Lombrado thought. Still the face of Don Vito betrayed nothing of his feelings, unless you could count a drawing down of the lower lip as a sign.

'Believe it,' Madonnia said, drawing himself upright. He knew he had it made now: he'd all but spat on the old goat and still nobody had taken the bait. He'd have it all around the streets in an hour, everyone would roll up just to shake the hand of the man who'd backed down Vito Ferro. Yet it had been so simple, so easy: one good push and the old goat had backed down. Still, what could you expect from a man who didn't even drink a full glass of wine with his whole meal?

Madonnia threw the three men a mocking salute, gave them a low bow, grinning as he bade them *arrivederci* and sauntered out of the Stella d'Italia like a man who'd just found ten thousand dollars.

Lombrado looked at Don Vito and saw what he had expected in Don Vito's eyes.

He muttered an excuse and rose from the table as Lupo let the breath out of his lungs in a long quavering sigh, so concerned with wondering how he was ever going to begin to apologize to Don Vito for the insults of his rebellious follower that he hardly noticed Lombrado leave.

'Don Vito,' he began, 'I — '

'No, no, Lupo,' Don Vito said. 'Contain yourself. The man was beyond all reason. We did all we could do. Let us speak of more important things. This letter of which Madonnia spoke: it must be retrieved, of course. That will be your task. I have no fear that you will disappoint me.'

Lupo nodded nervously, understanding quite clearly that he had been given a period of grace, nothing more. He bent low over the table to kiss Don Vito's hand, gabbling promises and gratitude.

'No, no,' Don Vito said, quietly. 'Come, Lupo, take another glass of wine. Let us talk about more pleasant things. Look, its only ten o'clock. A game of cards, perhaps. What do you say?'

The unexpectedness of Don Vito's camaraderie took Lupo aback for a moment and then he realized for the first time that Lombrado had still not come back to the table. A sudden blank chill enveloped him. He looked at Don Vito Cascio Ferro and realized why his attention had been drawn to the time, why Don Vito had suggested another glass of wine, a lingering game of cards. And why Antonio Lombrado had not come back to the table.

'Deal,' Don Vito said, handing him the cards.

★ ★ ★

They let Madonnia get as far as Bleecker Street.

It was very nicely set up, efficient and smooth, like everything that Antonio Lombrado handled. Two men coming towards Madonnia from the Bowery at the same time that two others came up behind him, their meeting point the preselected *cul-de-sac* half-way along the block between Elizabeth Street and the Bowery, on Bleecker. Madonnia wasn't aware of them at first, but when they got near enough, they let the dog see the rabbit. The two men approaching Madonnia drew knives from the sheaths inside their coats, and Madonnia saw the glint of steel and whirled about, poised, ready to run if he had to, but not frightened yet. Then the two men behind him produced their knives and his head came up, the shock showing in his eyes now. He looked in panicked haste across Bleecker, only to see Antonio Lombrado standing there, his hand in his overcoat pocket and — Madonnia had no doubt at all — a gun in that hand. So there was only one way for him to move and he moved, just as Lombrado had intended that he should move, into the darkness of the *cul-de-sac*, where a third pair of men stood waiting in the filthy shadows. Madonnia ran straight into their arms, and squealed like a trapped rabbit when he realized what he had done. He was a big man, a strong man, and he knew that his life depended on the fight he put up now, but the men who had him were big men, too, and had the advantage of Madonnia's terror. They held him easily until the others came, knives at the ready.

4

There were all sorts of derelicts on the streets of Manhattan. The do-gooders divided them into two kinds: the deserving poor and the rest. You could always tell the deserving poor. They were the ones who would starve genteelly to death in the hovels without being a nuisance. The rest, the beggars and whores and cripples and blind men and winos and street sparrows, were shameless. They came right out on the street and jammed their stinking poverty up your nose, and if you had business anywhere south of Fourteenth Street, anywhere near Union Square or downtown Broadway, you were going to be accosted by beggars every fifteen paces whether you liked it or not. Some of the beggars were, of course, genuine cripples; deformed, or unable to work because of the loss of a limb or eyesight or disease. Others — well, every decent person knew about the women who hired babies by the day, the better to wring your heart with their tale of woe. Everyone knew about the families that dressed their children in rags and sent them out to beg for money so they could stay in their tenements, stupid with cheap gin. Everyone was aware that worthless failures who would not work preferred to buy a few ratty penny shoelaces or boxes of matches and stand on corners importuning passers-by to pay a dime or a quarter for them. Decent people avoided them all like the plague, knowing that to succour them was merely to encourage them. And if, as occasionally one read, someone actually died on the street from deprivation, or starved to death in some Five Points hovel, well, no one could be blamed for that. There were institutions and charities to which such people could go if they were genuinely in need.

But the beggars were only one aspect of the dereliction you found on the streets. There were the rowdies and the street-gang toughs in their red neckerchiefs and their heavy boots, who'd knock you down

and rob you soon as look. There were the
whores; and, downtown, you saw few of
the elegantly dressed *demi-mondaines* of
Fifth Avenue and a great many more
whey-faced, pox-raddled travesties of
womanhood who would stoop to any
awful practice for a dollar or two. Then
there were the pickpockets who swarmed
on the streetcar lines, shameless in their
bravado. There were con-men and footpads looking for 'mugs', and on top of all
that there were street-vendors of all
shapes, sizes and sex, hawking watches
and trinkets and newspapers and fruit
and cigars and candies and cakes and
ice-creams and hot sausages and flowers
and birds and stationery and anything
else which could be sold from a pushcart
in the gutter or a tray or a box or a bag
or a basket. Soup or socks, oysters or
neckties, you can buy them all on the
packed sidewalks of the city. All of them,
the balloon men and the penny whistle
vendors, the ones who sell puppy dogs
and the ones who pull the strings of
the jumping-jacks are all of them,
men, women and children, among the

unemployed, the border-liners, the ones who won't work or can't work or would just as soon not work regularly, under a roof, for wages, like any civilized man.

All these, however, are the upper crust.

Beneath and below it, moving mostly unseen by the eyes of the daylight throngs, are the real derelicts. These are the river-rats, the Water Street winos, the grotesque pimps of the raddled whores in Cherry Street and Slaughterhouse Point, as the cops call the intersection of James and South Streets. In the Bowery gin mills and the Five Points bucket shops lived species of men and women that it was probably as well the decent folk of Manhattan rarely saw. By day they were hidden away in some alley somewhere, buried under a mound of newspapers or shivering in some abandoned tenement that even the rats had given up on. They came out at night, looking for the warmth at the bottom of a bottle of rotgut hooch, the fellowship of men and women as spaced out as themselves, the bums, the vags, the winos, the floozies and the goners.

Peter Nash wasn't quite a goner, but he was damned close to it. A shambling, tatterdemalion figure, vacant-eyed and crooning, his brain long since seared clean of memory by the stuff he poured down his throat, Peter Nash looked like a bundle of rags that had got up and started moving about. He wore a series of ragged coats, the outer one of which had once boasted a fur collar that now looked as if Nash had the remains of a decomposed cat around his neck. His string-tied boots — if you could call what he had on his feet boots — gaped where the destroyed soles had parted from the cracked, torn, whitened uppers. His filthy, unsocked feet peered from inside the boots, which he had packed with newspaper, and his gingery, ragged beard and graying hair were matted and unkempt. His eyes had the wary cunning of a cornered stoat.

He stank.

Not that it mattered; in the kind of company Peter Nash kept, such niceties meant nothing at all. If you had a bottle, you smelled sweeter than all the perfumes of Araby. A bottle was a passport to

Nirvana, a solution to all life's problems. A bottle meant not caring where you laid your head, since you would be unconscious, heedless of cold stone or biting wind. A bottle meant taking the sharp edge of the daylight away, removing the world, substituting a twilit, happy place. So it was the thought of how to get enough money to buy a bottle which remained constantly uppermost in Peter Nash's mind.

To the really serious drinker, and Peter Nash was about as serious as they come, lack of funds is not so much a tragedy as a challenge. With no funds at hand to buy his food, his drink, his meat, his potatoes, his rosy nirvana — liquor — the burnt-out mind which any doctor would have instantly pronounced worthless would suddenly blossom into fertile originality. Your wino, your vagrant, your stumbling bum would don a lurching gentility, hustling passers-by for pennies, thanking them for nothing with a staggering bow, obscenely polite, that might well end in a reeling grab at the mark's lapels. And many a strong man would hand over all his loose change as fast as he could get it out of his pocket in order to escape the devastating puissance of the wino's breath. Another way was to perform a song or a dance or both in the street. You'd often see a drunk on Broadway dancing to music he alone could hear, leering ingratiatingly at pedestrians and unconscious of the curses of the cabbies and the streetcar drivers as they whizzed past his reeling figure.

However, neither of those was any good to Peter Nash.

To begin with, it was too early. He hadn't scored last night and so he hadn't slept at all, walking the streets from about dawn because he'd been shivering too much to sleep. The few workmen who would be on the streets at this hour were not the kind you could hustle for pennies. Many of them were Irish, and some of them would kick your head in just to get the day started properly. Six o'clock in the morning on East Eleventh Street was neither the time nor the place to raise the wind for a cutter. And with the squeezing pain in his belly and the taste of a fish-gutter's apron in his mouth, Peter Nash needed a drink more than any single thing in the whole wide world.

Even though the cumulative effect of drinking for years rotgut booze which would literally have killed a cow, Peter Nash still instinctively observed the wino's survival rule: use what is available, get what you can, and only steal when you have to. Not that he gave a damn for the moral aspects of thieving. It was just that inside the Tombs, the do-gooders got at you and tried to get you better. And the first thing they did was to keep you away from the stuff. So he racked what was left of his brain for an idea. Too early, for instance, to wander along Fourteenth Street and see what he could steal off the barrows or the display stands outside the shops where goods, garments, food, hung in inviting profusion. You could pick up an apple here, another there, half a dozen apples and then over to Union Square and sell them for a quarter. Or maybe a bottle of vinegar or a wooden spoon or a cheap tie: anything that you could convert to money in one of the open spaces downtown, City Hall Park for instance, or outside the newspaper offices in Nassau Street. Too early to hustle, too early to steal: the only thing left was to scavenge, and Peter Nash was an expert at that.

Garbage dumps, refuse heaps, back alleys where the overflowing trash cans stood reeking, the glutinous shorelines of the river — he knew how to comb them, all right, how to battle with the cats and the unpanicking rats for the things discarded by those more fortunate or more careless than he. You'd be surprised what you sometimes found in trash cans, but it's probably the kind of surprise you're happy to do without. Peter Nash wasn't so picky: he needed the price of a drink and if that was how he had to raise it, then he'd raise it that way.

Nodding, determined, and with a destination in mind, he headed along Eleventh Street towards the Bowery for all the world like an old newspaper blown before a fresh Atlantic breeze. He sang a melody inside his head that emerged from his cracked lips as an appalling whine, his rheumy eyes scouring the darker corners behind the tenements for a promising garbage pile. He turned off the street and into an alley, heading for the narrow gap in the building that gave access to the airshaft. Although it was against every law and city ordinance that had ever been invented, the people who lived in the tenements tipped their garbage out of the windows. After all, who needed the walk down six or seven flights of stairs with a trash can in your hands, only to find when you got down to the street that the refuse collectors hadn't been and there was no place to put your garbage anyway? Everything went out of the windows that the inhabitants didn't need; sometimes, even, the inhabitants themselves.

It was pretty dark in the alley, even though the first striated hints of morning were lightening the sky. Peter Nash tended to forget what his intention was if he let his concentration wander even a little, so he kept his eyes riveted on the destination he had in mind, the overflowing garbage pails in back of the tenement. That way he didn't see the barrel until his hip bumped into it and reeled off it the way a pool ball will angle away from the cushion. He sat down heavily, frowning with concentration, glaring at the barrel. Something was wrong with it and he couldn't think what it was. Then he knew: the damned thing must be heavy if it had knocked him over rather than the other way round. Which meant it was full.

Now what in the name of God was a full barrel doing sat smack in the middle of an alley between two tenements? A barrel was not just a barrel down here. It could be firewood. It could be storage. It could be something to sell. It could be money on the table from half a dozen draymen or stores. You could get ten dollars for a barrel if it was a good one and this was a good one and so it shouldn't be here at all. You put a barrel down anywhere around this part of the world and walked away from it for five minutes, it was gone, man. You wouldn't see anyone, hear anything; but that barrel would be gone as clean as if someone had vapourized it. Ask fifty people standing around and not one of them would have seen a damned thing.

Which meant the barrel hadn't been here long, Peter Nash figured. Which meant he had a chance of moving it away before the neighbourhood awoke, which was going to be pretty soon. He got up and lurched over to the barrel, setting his weight firmly on his feet and trying to tilt the barrel to an angle which would enable to get it on the edge and roll it down to the end of the alley and on to the pavement. He was sweating and the morning breeze chilled his body.

The barrel was unmarked except for the letter WT burned into it at the belly. The top was nailed down. Could be anything, he thought. Salt, maybe, even a pork barrel. If it was a pork barrel and it was full — it felt like it was full, by God! — then it had been stolen and left there and that meant someone was going to come back for it and he had to get it away from here soon. It was also pure gold, because it was worth twenty dollars anywhere on the Bowery. The German butchers down there would give you twenty quick as a wink, no questions asked, for a barrel full of salted pork. All he had to do was get it down there. He did a little jig of triumph around his trophy.

'Twenty bucks,' he chanted to himself. 'Twenty bucks.'

He shook his head at his own luck, checked the street both ways to make sure there were no cops in sight, and laid hands on the barrel again. It was damned heavy, all right, he thought, panting, bracing himself against the weight. He started to roll it down towards the Bowery and as he did his foot went from under him, betrayed by a sodden wodge of pulped newspaper lying on the littered sidewalk. For an awful moment he thought the barrel was going to crush him to death, and he kicked out with his feet from the ground, jarring his whole body but succeeding in turning the wobbling barrel away from his sprawled figure.

The barrel rolled over in what seemed like a ponderously slow movement, making a sound like *wrong-wurrong-wrong* as it half-turned, moving faster gradually, bouncing off a fire hydrant and then rolling off the pavement and into the street. The seven-inch drop jarred the lid off the top of the barrel, which swung round with the open end towards Peter Nash and came to a stop against the parapet of the sidewalk. Peter Nash shook his head, not believing what he saw. There was a man in the barrel.

A dead man.

He got on to his hands and knees and crawled across the pavement towards the barrel, now uneasily halted. His ratty eyes were none too sharp and he had to get fairly close in order to be able to see properly in the iron-grey light of the dawn. Then he saw clearly what had been done to the man in the barrel and he screamed.

It wasn't a short, sharp, piercing screech, the kind they were used to — and usually completely ignored — on these downtown streets. It wasn't the terrified squeal of a molested woman: God knows, they got enough of those, as well. It was a long, aching, extenuated sound of astonished terror that went on and on, bringing men and women to the noisily raised windows of the tenements, a scream that went on and on and on until Peter Nash turned up his eyes and went over on the pavement in a dead faint, his head hitting the sidewalk with a sound they could hear on the eighth floor above.

It took the police twelve minutes to arrive and by that time there was a crowd of around two hundred people jostling for a chance to see the dead man in the barrel with his genitals stuffed in his mouth.

5

The average Federal law-enforcement officer doesn't have a great deal of time for, or patience with, the City or State variety of policeman. The Federal law-enforcement officer sees a broad picture of crime on a national scale, where the city cop has his nose stuck in the tramline of his own beat. There's an elitism involved, too: the Federal law-enforcement officer is free of, and glad that he is free of, the politically orientated machine which makes the life of most metropolitan policemen hell. Of course, you could also argue that they didn't have to sit still for it; you could argue that those who did sit still did so because in fact they enjoyed the privileges of the machine, and the various perks which came from being a part of it. That was a pretty sour view, of course, but watching Inspector David Schmittberger handling the 'man in the barrel' case, Flynn wasn't prepared to argue it on any academic basis. The man was a charlatan, pure and simple. Here he was, in charge of the entire Second Inspection District of the City of New York, and he patently couldn't unbutton his own fly without an instruction book.

To explain: The New York Police Department is divided into sixty-four precincts. Half of these were in the First District, the other half in the Second, each district under the direct control of an inspector of the NYPD. So in other words, an inspector had nominal control of thirty-two precincts, in turn run on a day-to-day basis by a police captain. These thirty-two captains each had four sergeants to manage the actual running of the Precinct House. To save you doing the arithmetic, that means that an inspector had charge of thirty-two captains, one hundred and twenty-eight sergeants, and various other special ranks, and if you take into account the fact that there were two districts, and therefore double that number of officers in a total force of around three thousand policemen, you can understand why sometimes the low-paid patrolman pulling the dirtier end of a beat no inspector or captain had even seen for a decade sometimes came up with the unoriginal idea that what the NYPD needed was fewer chiefs and more Indians. Especially when there were forty patrolmen on permanent court duty, and another fifty-odd in charge of the sanitary squads — it being one of the NYPD's special privileges, courtesy Hizzonner the Mayor, to supervise the collection of the island's garbage. No one had successfully explained to any cop just what this had to do with law-enforcement, but since there was obviously a fat buck in it for someone somewhere, what could you do? Go fight City Hall, they said. It just seemed sometimes that the beat men did all the grafting and the brass took all the graft, if you took the point. It was a philosophy Flynn had heard plenty of times on the streets, and it made it all the more surprising — at first — that Schmitt-berger had taken personal charge of a case that had all the outwards signs of being a very hot potato. The body of the 'man in the barrel' had been found in the Second District, sure, and that made it his nominal responsibility. But Schmittberger taking personal control was something else, and it wasn't, as some of his almost entirely disloyal staff suggested, because the Inspector felt some affinity with the corpse, being a man who spent a lot of the time making about as much sense as someone with his cock in his mouth.

Flynn realized pretty soon that Schmittberger had taken over for one reason and one reason only: to get rid of the case, pass it on, hand it over, lose it. If he gave the case to one of his detectives, it would linger around the Second District like a wheedling wino. You'd never get rid of it, or the newspapers or the Commissioners or the Mayor, all of whom were demanding a rapid solution to this ugly murder. If, however, he gave orders to someone else, who could argue with him? He also knew, Flynn figured, that if he passed the 'man in the barrel' along to a specialist, he would also get Flynn off his back, and Flynn was beginning to think he'd like that very much indeed. He just plain didn't get along with the Inspector.

Schmittberger was a rotund, jowly man of about fifty-five who looked as if he'd never taken any exercise heavier than lifting a forkful of food as far as his thick-lipped mouth. He was about as subtle as a stampeding horse and over the time that Flynn had been dealing with him, he'd learned his favorite expression was 'Don't argue with me!' Accent on the 'me'. He just plain didn't know what the hell to do with the barrel killing.

The usual way to get ID — identification — was to put the corpse on display in the City Morgue up at Bellevue, but that was impossible now, because the newpapers had stirred up public curiosity to such an extent that they'd have a riot over there if they did. Of course, the papers hadn't actually put into one-syllable words what by now half the city knew the condition of the corpse to have been when found; but more than enough. No doubt Schmittberger would have admitted — if only to himself — that he didn't have the first idea of how to establish the dead man's identity or come up with a motive for his macabre murder. He seemed to be inclining — Flynn entered a demurrer to which he replied 'Don't argue with me!' — to one newspaper's theory that it might be some kind of ritual murder. After all, he said, there were enough East Europeans in Manhattan now for anything to be possible. Flynn heard he had people checking everywhere for the name of a secret society which might have the initials JNJR. These had been engraved on a cross found on the dead man. The only thing in the possession of the corpse other than the cross was a scribbled note in Italian, and it was all David Schmitt-berger needed.

'We'll hand it over to the Dago!' he said.

Flynn knew who the Dago was, of course. Everyone did. It was a byword at Police HQ and in a number of other places which might have surprised the Commissioners, that anything connected with Italian crime — on the teeming streets of Little Italy or anywhere else

— was the eminent domain, not to say the sole prerogative, of Joe Petrosino. Or the Dago, as they called him. But not, Flynn noticed, to his face.

Flynn asked around, tried to find out all he could about him. His reputation was enormous: if he couldn't find out whatever it was you wanted to know about the Italians, nobody could. And not only that — when he set about it, he found things out quicker than anyone else in Manhattan, and that included the Chief of Police, the Commissioners and the goddamn Mayor himself. Other detectives spoke his name with awe, recounted his exploits with a kind of astonishment in their voices that made Flynn wonder whether Petrosino was really that good, or whether he had the entire NYPD psych'ed out of its collective mind. There was one other thing about Petrosino that became immediately apparent when Flynn talked with the boys at Mulberry Street: they all cordially hated his guts.

To begin with, he was a nut.

It's no bad thing to have a fixation.

Whatever you can imagine, however bizarre, that the underworld is up to, you're probably right. But Petrosino! He believed that every murder that happened in Manhattan — or for that matter the entire goddamn US of A — was due to a closely knit, cohesive fraternity of Italian gangsters. 'Oh, come on,' Flynn had said, protesting. 'Well,' they said, hedging a little, 'if it involves anyone with an Italian background, with a name that sounds half like it might be Italian' (they pronounced it Eye-tally-ann) 'then you can bet a week's pay that Petrosino will claim it's his secret society at work.'

His secret society?

'Yeah, sure,' they told Flynn. 'His own personal, special, secret society. Only he knows anything about it. The reason being that he don't tell nobody nothing about it. Nobody: not the Commissioners, not the Chief, nobody.' Now that was hard enough to take, Jesus, even if he was a Lieutenant now, especially when you harked back, like some of the older members of the Department, to the fact that Petrosino had started his career with the police as an informer. Hard enough to take, but not half as hard as when he started telling you that it was his secret society who'd arranged for the assassination of the King of Italy. When he started talking to the newspapers (and they, whether they believed him or not, printed what he said: Joe was always good copy) about how he'd warned President McKinley that he was going to be assassinated — well, then you just had to hold up your hands in a defensive position and say okay, okay, Joe baby, and get the hell out of there.

Flynn tactfully refrained from pointing out to them that Petrosino's work with the anarchists, whom he'd joined undercover, had indeed turned up a plot to assassinate McKinley which had been ignored higher up. So far no one had come up with a theory about why anyone would have wanted to shoot down the harmless President that was any better than Petrosino's, but he didn't say that either. He understood how cops felt. If it had been any other of their number saying all this to the *World* and the

Tribune, they'd have been delighted. But it wasn't anyone else, it was that goddamned egomaniac Joe Petrosino, the nut, the loner, the one who didn't swing with the system. There'd been a time, so the scuttlebutt in the Department went, when Joe Petrosino had been a hell-for-leather cop of the best kind, working as an undercover man with a price put on his head by the racketeers down in Little Italy. He'd worked in saloons, and on the docks, in meat-packing plants and markets, getting to know all the gang bosses and the ward-heelers, all the fixers and the muscle-men, the Black Hand bomb throwers and extortion experts, feeding back his findings to NYPD in the shape of the then Chief of Detectives, Inspector Tom Byrnes. There'd been an almost father-son relationship between the big Irishman and the thickset, short, black-eyed Italian, which had become stronger during the years of Petrosino's undercover work, and which had ended on the day they caught Tom Byrnes, 'the unfixable cop', with his hand in the cash register.

It was hard for anyone to believe that the man who'd established the celebrated 'deadline' at Fulton Street — below which no known criminal was permitted to venture downtown — had 'taken his pigeon from Delmonico's' like the cheapest Tammany grafter. The outcry was enormous. Wasn't this the man who'd dealt quietly with the blackmail cases of the Four Hundred and the monied brokers of Wall Street? Wasn't this the supercop who'd known personally, by sight, every criminal, every footpad, every fence operating in Manhattan? If he was bent, what hope for the ordinary citizen? And if it was a shock to New Yorkers in general to discover that Tom Byrnes was no better than he had to be and a damned sight worse than he'd any right to be, think of the effect on Petrosino when Byrnes was busted. It was the ultimate betrayal.

He had risked his life, daily, to obtain information from the streets of Little Italy, and Byrnes had passed it over to his Tammany bosses indiscriminately. Had it not been for the fact that the politicians found Joe's information useful to them in many, many, other ways and wanted to keep it coming in, he would have been a dead man. But he was never betrayed because without him there was no way of getting that kind of information. Little Italy was closed to anyone who wasn't *paisan*, an Italian.

It wasn't so much a place enclosed within certain geographical boundaries as a state of mind, an attitude. It didn't stretch from this Avenue to that street. It was Italy, like Naples was Italy and Florence was Italy, transported in grubby sacks and rattan suitcases, leather valises and steamer trunks across seven thousand storm-tossed, flea-bitten, retching, sweating, jam-packed, poverty stricken, miles of ocean in the stinking steerage of immigrant steamers. It survived the ritual disgrace of Ellis Island and Castle Garden, it survived the traitorous *padrone* system that sold its sons into near-slavery, it survived the alien land and the even more alien people, and it survived being surrounded by the ghettos of a polyglot mix of its racial and instinctive enemies: Jews, Slav, Pole,

German and Irish. It was place where you spoke your own tongue, your own dialect; followed your own ways; lived the life you had always lived, except that you did it now in a country where the people knew nothing of oppression, nothing of plague, nothing of famine or feudalism, and neither understood those who still feared them or cared either way. Here in their own *quartiere*, they were safe.

Here they drank the good Italian wines, and slowly others learned to do the same. Here they ate the old Italian foods, and gradually others found that they were good. So a man could make a living with a store, a café, or a restaurant, remaining still Italian among this volatile, pungent, kaleidoscopic mix of Italians as illiterate as he, as voluble as he, as displaced as he, all crowded together in the ghetto that they had themselves erected so that only someone Italian could ever begin to fathom its ways. Only if he were Italian could he probe deep, ask questions. Only if he, like they were part of that astonishing movement of people which brought Italy to the streets of lower

Manhattan, part of a world phenomenon: two and a half million in the seventies, another five million in the eighties, yet another four million in the next decade landing in New York alone.

Only someone like a Petrosino could understand it.

Only a man who could sweat alongside his *paisan* in the fish market, swinging the slimy wooden boxes of bass and skate and herring on to the high-backed drays until his spine felt as if someone had been hacking at it with an axe could understand. Only a man who relaxed the same way everyone else did, with a good glass of wine, or *grappa* if he'd got the pennies, only a man who smoked your kind of cigarettes and played the same games you both learned in the same kind of dusty square in Naples, or Salerno, Messina, Palermo, or some smaller, dustier village then even those. Only a man who spoke your language with the same lilt, the same inflexions, the glutinous gutturals of the Sicilian dialect or the caressing vowels of the Neapolitan.

If you were a street-vendor, say, who

could appreciate your problems the way another street-vendor could? The daily grind of heaving the half-ton pushcart through garbage-garnished gutters, kicking out a clear pitch amid the smelly debris of yesterday, jostling for a good location opposite the most patronized stores, hawking the bits and pieces which you'd risen at dawn to bid for at the markets, shouting to attract custom until you were speechless, watching the street clocks whose fingers relentlessly brought down your prices, until at the end of the day the women came out of the tenements in hordes, flies buzzing over the offal of what was left on the pushcarts when everyone else was through buying. If you ended your day with a back that ached like a coal-heaver's, a couple of dollars ahead and nothing to look forward to but doing it over the following day, who could understand how you felt except someone like yourself. *Ai, paisan,* who else?

After dark, when the gaslamps flared and you'd trudged down to Fulton Street to stack your barrow ready for the dawn, then walked back up to Little Italy, maybe you'd stop off for a beer, a glass of wine, and talk about what you had seen on the streets, and what you'd heard, and who you'd seen, and what they'd done.

You had to be a Petrosino to hear such things.

All the time, from the very earliest days when he'd worked in a saloon on Prince Street, later when he'd humped fish in the markets, worked as a coal-heaver, a dock-walloper, peddled fruit off a push-cart, had a job in a brokerage house, as a garbage collector, he'd been working on his own project. Keeping meticulous notes in a series of black notebooks. He knew the names, and the descriptions that went with the names, and the rackets that went with both. The dock czars, the brothelkeepers, the anarchists and extor-tionists, the bunco artists and the bomb throwers, all carefully kept up to date and diligently cross-referenced. He designed his own forms, his own card indices, his own records, as he pursued the member-ship, the activities, and the background history of the special thing of the

Sicilians, the *alianza*, the clan society they saluted when they drank. 'Alla mamma!' they would chorus, or 'Alla madre nobile!' — meaning, not just their own mothers, but motherhood itself, the holy state, custodian of tradition, donor of life. And, he became sure later, to the place of their birth, the place where their roots lay forever buried: Sicily, whose coarse dialect was the only one they spoke among themselves.

You needed a Petrosino to understand that, too.

Giuseppe Michele Pasquale Petrosino, his father had christened him in the baking August heat of the little church at Padula, outside Salerno; Giuseppe for himself, for his father, for all the Petrosinos as far back as you cared to go had named their firstborn son Giuseppe; Michele Pasquale for the child's god-father, a farmer with whom the new father had gone to school in Corleone, a little hillside village in central Sicily. So Giuseppe had brought up his son with that special native knack of the tongue, speaking Sicilian as though born there, while the child himself learned Neapolitan and Salerno dialects on the streets, in the school. If it had been preordained that some individual be born to watch, to infiltrate the *alianza*, he could have been given no greater gift than his ability to speak those two dialects so naturally. Giuseppe Petrosino had come to New York as a boy; his parents had used the money from the sale of the farm to buy a little grocery store over on Hester Street, just east of the Bowery. Giuseppe, who soon Americanized his name to Joe as he painfully learned to speak the language of his new country, lived there with them over the store for years. Until the Tom Byrnes fiasco, in fact.

After that, Petrosino came out from undercover and never went back. He let them see him in his uniform and the men who had confided in their *paisan* now spat in his path, for what he had done was an *infamità*, a betrayal of the worst kind. They made up jokes about his name, which meant 'parsley' in American, or about his size, for he was not a tall man. They made slighting remarks about his appearance, for he was pockmarked from childhood smallpox, and beginning to go bald.

The more they insulted him, the more determined, the more dedicated, the more unapproachable he became. His arrest record was second to none. He buried himself in his work, gnawed at it, worried over it, fretted when it was not done, sought more long before he had finished what he was doing. Such contacts as he had with his parents languished. Friendships formed in the *quartiere* dissolved. He had no confidant on the Force and seemed to want or need none. He lived alone and lonely by choice, sleeping as often as not on a cot in the office they had given him on the fourth floor of the Mulberry Street building where he specialized in matters Italian. His company, when he had company, was thieves seeking a deal, pimps sharing a secret, informers turning in dubious betrayals in return for greasy five-dollar bills. His colleagues regarded him first with awe, then astonishment that turned slowly to sour disinterest, and finally with something close to pity. *Pazzo*, they said, mimicking his Italian-ness. Crazy as a bedbug.

Well, Flynn reckoned, Petrosino was a lot of things, but crazy wasn't one of them. He knew from his own work that Petrosino was right, that there was indeed some kind of secret society, an alliance that called itself the Mafia. Unlike Petrosino, however, he did not believe that the Great American Public was ready for the information yet. They didn't want to believe that such a thing could exist in the home of the brave and the land of the free. They didn't want to know that they were being used, manipulated, indirectly taxed by the cost of the crimes the *mafiosi* committed. One day, perhaps, they would. One day, when they had had their noses rubbed into it so fiercely that it would be impossible to pretend otherwise. But that day was a long way away, and in the meantime, the more Petrosino tried to make the GAP face up to itself, the more it would shy away. The same went for politicians, Chiefs of Police, and everyone else: they wouldn't make any great effort until the GAP kicked their fat asses for them. One day they would. When that day came, they'd need a Petrosino.

Meantime, it was plain that they were happy to 'lose' certain cases by handing them over to the Italian Branch, just as Inspector David Schmittberger was doing with the 'man in the barrel.' Flynn was just as glad to be shut of Schmittberger as the Inspector was to be rid of him, he guessed. They hardly spoke as they rattled across town in the police vehicle. Schmittberger led the way into the echoing hall of the Mulberry Street building, nodding in response to the smart salute of the parolman at the foot of the ornate staircase. They went up to the fourth floor, and Schmittberger led the way through a warren of corridors with faceless half-glassed doors behind which Flynn could hear the clack of typewriters, the occasional persistent shrill ring of a telephone. Petrosino's office was at the far end of a dusty side corridor, its door as anonymous as the rest. Schmittberger opened it without knocking and the man at the desk facing the door swung around to face them.

He was just the way he'd been described, Flynn thought. Wide, sloping shoulders. Square face, straight nose, ears set close to the head. Noticeable double chin. Thin upper lip, almost straight, over fuller lower lip. Level, almost lashless eyes. Skin heavily pockmarked but strangely unlined. Petrosino was wearing a white soft-collared shirt and an open blue serge waistcoat held together by a heavy gold watch-chain. His detective's shield with the number 285 was pinned to the lapel of the waistcoat on the left. He rose to shake hands, and Flynn realized that Petrosino couldn't be more than five foot seven or eight. He hadn't ever thought of himself as tall and slim, but that was the way he felt as he stood facing Joe Petrosino for the first time.

After they'd dispensed with the introductions and the preliminaries, the two visitors pulled chairs in front of Petrosino's desk and got down to business. Or rather, Schmittberger did. Flynn sat quietly and watched; listening, noticing

that from time to time Petrosino's eyes
flicked towards him, weighing, assessing,
All he's got is the name, William Flynn,
and the rank, Special Investigator,
Department of Justice. So that puts him
on the defensive, makes him uncertain.
Let him stay that way awhile, Flynn
thought.

'Why me?' Petrosino was asking Schmittberger.

'Hell, Joe,' Schmittberger said. 'We
figured if anyone could make a hole in
this case the Da — Joe Petrosino was the
one to do it.'

If the man behind the desk noticed
Schmittberger's near slip of the tongue,
he didn't react. Probably knows damned
well what they call him behind his back,
Flynn thought.

'What's your thinking?' insisted Petrosino,
making Schmittberger work for it, and
enjoying making him. He acted like a
man well aware of the fact that the
Inspector hated even being here, let alone
admitting he couldn't get anywhere with
the case.

'Well,' Schmittberger said, taking a

DOA report out of his inside pocket.

'The coroner says what we've got is a white male, approximately thirty years of age, who had been stabbed to death with one or more long-bladed knives with blades one inch across. Probably stilettos. The body was then mutilated by cutting off — '

'I know about that,' Petrosino said abruptly. 'How many times was he stabbed, and where, exactly?'

'Seven times,' Schmittberger told him. 'In the throat and chest mostly. One shot in the belly. Doc Hagen says any one of four of the wounds would have been fatal.'

'Clothes?'

'Just shirt and pants, socks, shoes. Not a label on any of them.'

'Uhuh,' Petrosino said. He was making notes on a pad. 'Go on. Description?'

'Height, six two,' Schmittberger read from the dead-on-arrival report. 'Weight, two hundred eight pounds. Hair, sandy blond, receding. Eyes, green.'

'So?' Petrosino said, leaning back in his chair.

You bastard, Flynn thought. You're enjoying pushing Schmittberger into trotting out his own ideas so that you can shoot them down in front of me.

'Well,' the Inspector said reluctantly. 'We were kind of working on the idea that it was some sort of ritual murder. There's a lot of Russians and Polacks in town these days, and that cross we found with the initials on it, you know, made us figure he might have belonged to some secret society, something like that?'

'You got it with you?'

Schmittberger nodded and reached into his jacket pocket. He took out a flimsy envelope, from which he shook on to Petrosino's desk a crucifix and chain. The cross was perhaps an inch and a half long; it caught a stray ray of sunlight from the window. Petrosino reached across with the air of a man who is being put upon, sliding the crucifix towards him with a thick finger.

'Boy!' he said. 'That's some secret society.'

'What?' Scmittberger snapped, hearing only the sarcasm in Petrosino's tone.

'I said that's some secret society,' Petrosino said. 'The Catholic Church.' His slow smile was almost deliberately provocative, the smile of a smart-ass punk kid. Well, thought Flynn, I'm getting a crash course in understanding why the NYPD has never thrown Petrosino a testimonial dinner.

'All right,' Schmittberger said, tightly. 'All right, go on.'

'JNJR,' Petrosino said, a patient parent explaining a simple sum to a backward child, 'stands for *Jesus Nazarenus Rex Judaeorum*. Jesus of Nazareth, King of the Jews. Which means your stiff was a Catholic. And which gets us precisely nowhere. What about the note?'

'I — how'd you know about the note?'

'It was in the papers,' Petrosino said impatiently. 'Like everything else you've told me so far. Did you bring it with you?'

Schmittberger took a folded piece of paper out of his wallet and laid it flat on the desk, smoothing it out with his fingers.

'Hm,' Petrosino said.

'Not much use, huh?' Flynn said,

speaking for the first time.

'Not much,' Petrosino said, giving him a long look. 'You speak Italian?'

'Enough to be able to read that,' Flynn said. 'Mean anything to you?'

'Not a damned thing,' Petrosino said. ''The meeting will be at seven. Be punctual.' This all you've got?' His question was addressed to Schmittberger, who shrugged.

'They're working on a couple of things up at the Lab. The stiff's clothes, stuff like that. And Flynn here has a couple ideas.'

'Stuff like what?' insisted Petrosino.

'Well, the barrel,' Schmittberger said. 'It's got the letters WT burned on it. There were traces of sugar inside it. I've got some of my people checking it out. They'll let you know direct if anything turns up. Then there was some sawdust in the cuffs of the dead man's trousers. The Lab boys say it's from a restaurant or a saloon. Traces of food and alcohol show up under the microscope.'

'Great,' Petrosino said, a word of sarcasm in the way he used the word. 'Now we know that the dead man took a drink or ate a meal some time in the thirty years before he died. Always supposing they were his own pants he was wearing. Did you take a photograph?'

'Sure,' Schmittberger said. His face was stiff with suppressed anger as he pushed a ten by eight glossy across Petrosino's desk. The Italian looked at the picture for several long moments. It showed the corpse stretched out full length on a trestle table in the Bellevue morgue.

'Pretty,' he said.

'Ain't it the truth,' Schmittberger rejoined.

Petrosino leaned back again in his chair and rubbed his chin reflectively. 'Well,' he said. 'It's a Mafia killing. That's for sure.'

Flynn glanced at Schmittberger, who grimaced at him as though to say, oh, Jesus, here we go: every time someone shows him a stiff, the Sicilians did it.

'What makes you think that it's a Mafia killing, Lieutenant?' Flynn asked.

'He's guessing,' Schmittberger said flatly.

'No,' Petrosino said. 'No guess. If you knew anything about the Mafia at all,

110

Inspector, you'd know that their classic punishment for anyone who talks too much is this.' He gestured at the photograph on the desk.

'The Mafia,' Schmittberger said. 'Again.'

'That's right.'

'Couldn't possibly be anyone else?'

'I hardly see how.'

'Then,' Schmittberger said, the thinly concealed thread of satisfaction clearly audible in his tone, 'it's all yours, Petrosino. You're the specialist, right? The Italian expert, right? Your, uh, department is here specifically to investigate crimes of Italian ethnic origin, isn't that correct?'

'In every way,' Petrosino said. Flynn noted with surprise that Petrosino was enjoying the duel almost as much as Schmittberger. He seemed to be taking positive pleasure in being handed the Second District's hottest potato.

'Then I'll bid you a fond farewell, Lieutenant,' Schmittberger grinned. 'You are now formally in charge of the 'man in the barrel' case. You coming, Flynn?' He stood, preparing to leave.

'Couple of things I'd like to discuss with the Lieutenant,' Flynn said. 'Might as well do it now.'

'Sure,' Schmittberger replied. If the expression on his face had been capable of translation into words, Flynn thought, it would have said 'you can talk to the crazy son of a bitch for the rest of your life if you like. Just don't expect me to sit here and listen is all.' Schmittberger got his hat and coat and went across to the door, opened it. He half turned, putting on the face of a man with very much more important things to do than stand here talking.

'I'll leave you to it, then,' he said.

'You do that,' Petrosino replied levelly.

'Yes,' Schmittberger said. 'Well, then.'

Petrosino didn't give him any damned help at all, and after a moment, the Inspector coughed abruptly, and pulled the door shut behind him. A little harder, Flynn thought, than was strictly necessary.

'Shit!' Petrosino said contemptuously. He slid open a desk drawer and produced a battered black briar pipe and a water-proof tobacco pouch. Flynn watched in silence as Petrosino jammed dark shag tobacco into the bowl of the pipe with practised movements, knowing that Petrosino was weighing him up, putting himself in the Lieutenant's place and thinking his thoughts. He would see a fairly husky thirty-five year old, Flynn knew, with a narrow, unremarkable face, heavy eyebrows, sandy brown hair, and green eyes. He would estimate, more or less correctly, that Flynn weighed around a hundred and sixty pounds soaking wet, and stood about five feet nine in his bare feet. Petrosino produced a box of wooden kitchen matches now, lighting the pipe and creating a huge cloud of strong smelling tobacco smoke at which he waved an ineffectual hand, something like an apologetic look on his face. The smoke hung in the dusty air like drifting cirrus cloud, its curling tendrils stinging Flynn's nostrils.

'Your own horse?' he asked politely.

Petrosino gave him a look of startled puzzlement and then he smiled. The smile changed his whole face, making him look quite youthful, far less stern and unbending.

'No,' he said. 'The kids collect it on the streets. I pay them ten cents a ton.'

'They're robbing you,' Flynn grinned.

'That'll be the day,' Petrosino said. 'You wanted to ask me something?'

'A lot of things,' Flynn said. 'But let me explain first. I'm with the Organized Crime and Rackets Division of the Department of Justice. Ever heard of it?'

'No,' Petrosino said. 'I haven't.'

Well, you needn't make it sound like you not only haven't heard of it, but can't imagine wanting to, Flynn thought.

'We've set up a national law-enforcement agency in Washington,' Flynn went on. 'The idea is to correlate every major crime, cross-reference it, index it. To assemble evidence, names, photographs. To put together a complete picture of crime in the USA against the day when the Justice Department will have its own investigative arm.'

'That's interesting,' Petrosino said. He said it the way someone might use the

114

words who'd just been shown a tin tray. Boy! Flynn thought.

'So,' he said, deciding to plunge. 'I'm going to ask you to open your files to me, Lieutenant.'

'By God!' Petrosino said, knocking the dottle out of his dead pipe and looking at Flynn as though he'd suddenly turned green. 'You've got your nerve, I'll say that. You're a real humdinger, you are.'

'Thanks,' Flynn said drily. 'You're not exactly a day at the beach yourself, you know that?'

For a moment, he thought he'd gone too far. Petrosino puffed himself up a little, as though getting ready to explode, and Flynn suddenly realized that he'd forgotten what everyone constantly forgot, that Petrosino was as Italian, as Sicilian as the criminals he pursued. *Ergo*, he was as vain, as childish-proud. He thought the same way they did, maybe even observed some of their laws for all Flynn knew. The edges might have been softened by his contact with America. How much, he was about to find out. The Italian's fleshy face couldn't hold the sour look any longer. The grin lurking beneath it broke through and Joe Petrosino smiled.

'Been a while since anyone talked to me like that' he said mildly.

'Probably good for you,' Flynn observed.

Petrosino nodded slowly, his eyes lively, as though he was enjoying himself and surprised to find that he was. Flynn began to realize that, despite his appearance, Petrosino was still quite a young man and began, too, to understand the formidable reputation. He reached into his inside pocket and brought out his own note-book. Everything in it was written in a numerical code. He didn't fancy it would stand the close scrutiny of a crypto-analyst, but it would certainly prevent any chance reader making head or tail of his notes. He riffled through the pages until he found the one he wanted.

'Want to read you some names,' he said. 'You just listen, okay?'

'Okay,' Petrosino shrugged.

'Ignazo Lupo,' Flynn read aloud. 'Gabriele Pantucci. Pietro Calvocoressi. Pelligrino Morano.' He looked up.

Petrosino was just looking at him, but his eyes were wider, his lips parted slightly.

'Did I say something wrong?' Flynn asked mischievously.

Joe Petrosino looked at him for a long moment, and then, as if coming to a decision, nodded. He turned around in his swivel chair, back to Flynn, fishing in his waistcoat pocket for a bunch of keys, one of which he used to open the door of the squat metal safe with the ornate brass facings which stood behind him. From inside the safe he lifted a metal dispatch case, which he laid flat on the desk. This in turn he opened, using another key on the bunch he had taken from his pocket. He opened the lid so that it stood like a barrier between him and Flynn. The Justice Department investigator could see nothing of the contents of the case.

'I have always worked alone,' Petrosino said, closing the lid of the case. He had a bundle of white cards, maybe five inches by three deep, indexed letters dividing them, clipped together with a bulldog fastener whose arms folded flat. He unclipped the fastener, riffled through the cards.

'Lupo,' he said. 'Yes, Ignazo Lupo. He controls the East side of Manhattan. He's nearly seventy now. Born in Cefalu, Sicily. Came to the States in 1879. *Capo-famiglia*. Specialities: the markets, the brothels in the Water Street area, blackmail, extortion. I have him down for eighteen murders, but I can't prove any of them.'

'What's this capofamily thing?'

'Lupo is the head of his family. His gang, if you like.'

'How about the others?'

'Gabriele Pantucci is dead,' Petrosino said. 'He died in April. He was the head of all of the *Mafiosi*, the boss of all bosses.'

'The others?'

'Pelligrino Morano I know. He's in charge of Brooklyn. Another *capo-famiglia*. You can see the files later. Calvocoressi I don't know.'

'Buffalo,' Flynn supplied. 'I've got some stuff on him you might find interesting. The others, too.'

'And the *consiglieri* — have you anything on them?'

'The who?'

'*Consiglieri*. It means counsellors, advisers. The second most important member of a Mafia family is the *consigliere*.' He shook his head and gave Flynn one of those looks that says 'how am I ever going to be able to explain all this if you don't even understand the terms of reference I'm using?'

Flynn gave a wry smile. 'You're giving me that look that says it's no use explaining things as complicated as this to a dummy like me,' he said.

'I am?' Petrosino asked. He fastened his file cards together, put them carefully back into their clip and then into the dispatch case. He locked the case and put it back in the safe, closing the door an then turning to face Flynn with an expression that said now what?

'Explain it to me,' Flynn said. 'Tell me how it works.'

'You don't want to hear that stuff,' Petrosino said. 'You'll wind up like everyone else, saying they ought to send

119

the little men in the white coats after me. *Petrosino, che dovrebbe essere attestato,*' he muttered in closing.

'Petrosino,' Flynn stumbled to translate, 'who ought to be certified?'

'That's right,' Petrosino said. But his expression had softened. 'You can speak good Italian.' His voice still expressed it in a way that seemed to say 'for an American' but Flynn was beginning to get the feeling that this unfortunate mode of speech was not the deliberately provocative insult it seemed. Petrosino's command of English wasn't as perfect as he fondly imagined. Naturally he wouldn't admit it to himself; equally naturally nobody was going to walk up to him and tell him. Result: he would come up with a marginally incorrect response and it would sound like an insult. Patience, William, Flynn told himself.

'Listen,' he said. 'You eat lunch? I'll buy you lunch and we can talk.'

'I usually have something in the office,' Petrosino said.

There he went again, Flynn thought. He meant it to be a simple statement of fact; it came out like a churlish turndown of Flynn's generosity.

'Come on,' he said. 'I'll take you to lunch. My treat.'

'All right,' Petrosino said. There was animation behind his eyes, like a kid who's not sure he's going on a treat but hopes to hell he is. 'Where shall we eat?'

'I don't know,' Flynn said. Then, with a grin: 'Hey! You like Italian food?'

Petrosino's smile broke through, and Flynn felt a glow of relief. For a while there, he thought, I had the feeling I was going to have to break a leg to get a laugh. They went on down the stairs to the street level.

6

Nobody knew where the word came from, or how the Mafia had begun, Petrosino told Flynn. There were plenty of legends, he said. Most of them were romantic guesses. None of them seemed more than faintly likely. There was one story that came straight out of Sicilian folklore: that in 1282, during the French domination of the island, a French soldier had raped a young girl. Her mother had run through the streets screaming for help, shouting *ma fia, ma fia*, my daughter, my daughter, whereupon the local men had butchered the soldier. Their action led to a revolt in Palermo which became known as the Sicilian Vespers. Hundreds of French soldiers were slaughtered: ambushed, stoned, stabbed, garrotted, killed by any means upon which the peasants could lay their hands. A romantic tale, Petrosino said, except that the word for daughter in

Italian was *figlia*, and even the slurringly thick Sicilian accent had never reduced it to *fia*.

Another legend which sprang from the same revolt, the Sicilian Vespers, suggested that the rallying cry of the insurgents was '*Morte alla Francia Italia anela!*' — death to the French, cries Italy! The initials were convenient, the idea of anyone shouting the words next to absurd. Besides which, why Italy, not Sicily?'

'Because then the initials wouldn't fit?' Flynn suggested.

'Right,' Petrosino nodded.

'What do you think the origins of the Mafia are, then?'

'African,' Petrosino replied. 'Certainly Moorish. There's a word in Arabic, *mafia*, which means a refuge, or a safe place. It could be that. The *alianza* has always had strong links with North Africa. Tunisia, Morocco. Places like that.'

'You've certainly gone into it deeply,' Flynn said. 'Tell me about the families — wasn't that what you called them?'

'Oh, that,' Petrosino said, leaning to

one side as the waitress placed the plate of steaming *lasagna* on the table in front of him. It was a pleasant, muggily warm, little place called the Luna Azura at the corner of Spring and Lafayette. Apparently — from the friendly smiles he got when he came in — Petrosino ate here often. Flynn noticed that his eyes followed the waitress as she went back towards the kitchen. Petrosino caught the tail end of Flynn's look and shrugged as if he'd been caught stealing cookies.

'Her name's Adelina,' he said. 'She's nice, huh?'

Flynn, who had honestly not even noticed the girl smiled.

'She certainly is,' he said.

'Yeah,' Petrosino said. 'Well. Enjoy the food.' He dug into his *pasta* like a man expecting a famine, and Flynn followed suit: it was plain that Petrosino didn't believe in eating and talking at the same time. The detective was finished long before Flynn had made much of a hole in the food on his plate, and he leaned back, dabbing his mouth with the napkin.

'What's the matter, Flynn?' Petrosino

asked. 'Don't you like the food here?'

'Sure, sure,' Flynn smiled. 'I'm a slow eater. Why don't you tell me about the families while I finish.' What he thought was: fantastic! Petrosino doesn't know he eats like a pig. He figures everyone else is a slow eater. Which is some ego, all right. Or maybe he's just old-fashioned, doesn't give a damn about anyone or anything.

'It's simple enough,' Petrosino told him, emptying his wine glass and refilling it. 'The families, the whole thing, they're organized like a private army. At the bottom of the ladder are the hangers-on, the errand boys, the people who do the dirty jobs the men of respect won't dirty their hands with. They're called *picciotti*. Then there are the rank and file of the *alianza*. They're the soldiers, and that's what they're called: *soldati*. They are *mafiosa* only in the sense that they are what they call 'connected.' Ten of them can choose one soldier to be their own chief, or *capo*. You with me so far?.

'Sure,' Flynn said.

'Good,' Petrosino said. 'Now then. All the *capos* in one area — let's say

Brooklyn, for argument's sake — get together and choose a leader for all of their gangs. He's called a *capofamiglia*, the head of the family. Got it?'

'Clear as crystal,' Flynn said. 'What's a *consigliere*?'

Petrosino looked at him for a moment, as though his patience was being exhausted. 'I told you that back at the office,' he said heavily. 'Remember?'

'So you did,' Flynn said. 'He's a counsellor, a right hand man, yes?'

'That's it,' Petrosino said.

'How many families you reckon there are altogether?'

'I don't know,' Petrosino admitted. 'I'd guess there's at least one in most major cities. The really big cities might have up to four or five.'

'But you know some exist for certain.'

'Oh, yes. In New York there are the East Side family, and the West Side, the Brooklyn, New Jersey, and Staten Island organizations. Some of these, of course are *Camorristi*.'

Flynn groaned theatrically. 'Not another secret society?'

'In fact, yes. But not secret, not the same,' Petrosino said. 'And they are weakening a lot. *Camorristi*, the men of the Camorra, are from Naples area. From Salerno, Napoli, Barra, Mori, Ischia. Not so powerful now as the Sicilians. They will either merge together or fight for domination.'

'Which do you think it will be?'

'I don't know. It depends on the new *capo di tutti capi*.'

'The one to succeed Don Gabriele Pantucci, you mean?'

'You remember well,' Petrosino said, 'when you want to.'

'I'm only stupid some of the time,' Flynn joked.

'I see,' Petrosino said, as if making a note of it, and Flynn got that reaction again: the man really gives offence without having the slightest intimation that he's doing it. Some people — most people, come to that — are gifted with a degree of intuition about other people and themselves. They can sense atmosphere, know that the vibrations aren't right, that the electricity flowing between them isn't creating the right magnetic field. It usually comes out as a feeling that the person to whom they are talking doesn't like them or is unsympathetic to their viewpoint. The Spanish had the best word for it: *simpatico*. Petrosino seemed to be completely lacking in any sense of intuition whatsoever. Which could be as much of an advantage as not, Flynn reflected, but it sure as hell would never make the man popular. Well, here we go again, he thought, wondering how come he was having to do all the work when he was the one with the information.

'Counterfeiting,' he said.

For all the reaction the word got from Petrosino, he might as well have said 'Tuesday'. Petrosino just looked at him.

'It's what I'm working on right now,' Flynn explained. 'My department.'

'Your department,' Petrosino repeated.

'We got word out of New Orleans that there was growing traffic in counterfeit money in the, ah, Italian communities,' Flynn persisted. 'New York, New Orleans, Pittsburgh.'

'The *alianza* doesn't ordinarily — '

Flynn held up a hand. 'Hear me out,' he said. 'Maybe they just got started. Anyway, we got the word. We went into our files to see who might be underneath the stone. We've got some good files, Joe,' he added. 'You'd enjoy going through some of them.'

Petrosino put an expression of judiciously mild interest on his face, although he couldn't conceal the eager light in his eye. But he wouldn't let it come out, Flynn realized.

'Could be,' Petrosino admitted. 'Could be.'

Flynn sighed. 'Anyway. We put investigators into the field: one in New Orleans, one in Pittsburgh, and me here in Manhattan; trying to pick up leads. It was Garrity in Pittsburgh who broke the case. He's Irish, and some of the Irish mob there put him on to the outfit that was doing the actual printing — the Irish don't take any too kindly to the Italians muscling in on their patch. You probably know that.'

'Of course,' Petrosino said. 'Go on.'

'Garrity found out that the counterfeiting operation was being run by five men. The leader was a guy named Giuseppe di Primo. Garrity told the Department, got permission for a raid on the print shop. Knocked off four of the five. The engraver, the one who'd actually made the plates for the five-spots they were printing, wasn't there. He got clean away. Garrity seemed to think he'd headed for New York, which was how I got into the act.'

'And Di Primo?'

'He took the fall. They all did. Never said a word. Except he told Garrity that he was well-connected, and that Garrity better keep looking over his shoulder from now on. Garrity jeered at him and Di Primo said, 'You laugh now, but you won't laugh when Lupo's boys are through with you.' '

Petrosino laid a hand on Flynn's forearm. 'He said that? He said 'Lupo'?'

Flynn nodded. 'We don't have an ounce of proof he said it,' he pointed out. 'But I sure as hell would like to get some, wouldn't you?'

'Where's Di Primo now?'

'In the pen,' Flynn said. 'Sing Sing. He drew a five-to-seven.'

'Finish your meal,' Petrosino said, waving to Adelina for a check. 'And let's get moving!'

'Huh?'

'You heard,' Petrosino said. 'We've got a train to catch.'

'Hold on just a damned minute!' Flynn spluttered. 'I'm not half through here yet.' He gestured towards his plate. 'What train, anyway?' he added as a desperate afterthought.

'Hudson River Railroad,' Petrosino said, getting up from the table. 'To Sing Sing. But we've got to make some phone calls first.'

Flynn pushed back his plate and stood up. 'I wasn't all that damned hungry, anyway,' he said, grinning.

'Don't let me rush you too much, now,' Petrosino told him.

'As if you'd do a thing like that,' Flynn said.

★ ★ ★

Cornelius Vanderbilt (1794–1877) never did make it into the higher echelons of New York society, but he did quite a lot of other things for Manhattan that the Four Hundred never even contemplated. Some of the things he did were great; others, well, not so great. Cornelius, you see, had begun his career as a Staten Island ferryman, so he learned early that there are certain things people simply have to pay for, and travelling is one of them and shipping goods is another. Once he had that theory firmly fixed in his noddle, Cornelius hardly put a foot wrong. He made a fortune by opening a transportation system from New York to the California goldfields (overland portage by way of Nicaragua) using his Hudson River steamboat company as security. By 1853, he was able to confidently boast that he was worth eleven million dollars, and eleven million dollars in 1853 had a considerably larger purchasing power than the same quantity have today, and even today nobody would say a man who had that many shin-plasters was exactly starving to death. Cornelius Vanderbilt's formidable wealth did nothing at all for his standing with New York's Upper Tendom — as those acid-tongued, supercilious Fifth Avenueites referred to themselves — and it could be that he felt slighted at being so pointedly overlooked in their invitation lists and dinner parties. So he began to devote a commendable amount of zeal — he was nothing if not extraordinarily energetic — to buying up the entire city of New York, no doubt figuring that if he could actually swing the purchase, the Upper Tendom would have to invite him to their soirées, otherwise he wouldn't allow them to be held in Manhattan. Unfortunately for Cornelius, the island of Manhattan had somewhat appreciated in value since the good old days when Peter Minuit had horn-swoggled the local Indians with sixty gulders and a bottle of booze, and even the Vanderbilt millions couldn't quite meet the going price. So he settled for buying as much of Manhattan as he could — which was a sizeable chunk — and then proceeded to parley. He was a financial whiz, and in no time at all he was buying stocks and bonds and then railroad companies, gambling establishments, and, once in a while, a politician or two. He owned the New York and Harlem Railroad, and the New York Central Railroad, and the Lake Shore & Michigan, and the Michigan Central, and the Canada Southern, and God alone knew what else. He owned — so that old liar, Reliable Authority, had it — a piece of Johnny Morrisey's club on 24th Street. He had a stableful of blooded livestock and enough fancy carriages to fill up half of the Easter Parade all on his own. He had a house as big as a French chateau on Fifth Avenue at 57th Street. He was as rich as Croesus. But he never got into Society, Never.

Maybe the old 'Commodore' didn't give a tinker's cuss at the end. Whatever the truth of it, he gave Manhattan one of its greatest gifts: rapid transit. Cynics might say — and since they were cynics, they invariably did say — that in fact rapid transit was Manhattan's gift to the Commodore, who patently made millions out of it, just as he and his robber-baron friends, Gould and Rockefeller, had made millions out of railroad and steamships and bullion companies for as far back as anyone seemed able to remember. But be all that as it may, you had to say there was cause for thanks in the fact that Vanderbilt had replaced the old railroad depot at Fourth Avenue and 26th Street. You no longer had to take seats, as travellers in former years had perforce to do, in a horse-drawn car which was pulled through the Fourth Avenue Tunnel (with attendant risk of robbery from the Croker gang which had its headquarters there) up to 42nd Street. There, the car had been coupled to a locomotive and away uptown you went, rattling hell-for-leather at positively hair-raising speeds along the elevated tracks above the seething streets. Now there was an imposing new terminal which straddled Fourth Avenue at 42nd Street, massive in red brick, pillared and porticoed, its ironwork painted white to resemble marble, its spacious frescoed waiting-rooms finished in varnished woods. It was called Grand Central Station, and even if it was anything but

135

central for most New Yorkers, it was grand enough for anyone. The enormous glass-roofed train-shed now served as a terminus for every train entering and leaving the city — sometimes as many as a hundred in a single day. From Grand Central you could take a train for anywhere in the country that railway lines ran to, or one of the 'locals' that lurched noisily uptown, stopping every six or eight blocks. Like the one that Petrosino and Flynn took to Sing Sing.

★ ★ ★

Actually, there's no such place.

The name of the town in which the penitentiary stands is Ossining, which is in turn derived from the original Dutch name, Sinsing, which appears on maps dated 1656 drawn by Adriaen van der Donck and is probably all anyone would ever want to know about that. The village itself was pleasant enough in its wooded vale, but the frowning penitentiary on the high ground outside it seemed to throw a gloomy shadow across the place. And every man who'd anything to do with the law — whichever side of it he stood upon — knew the place by its nickname: Sing Sing.

The train journey was quite a spectacular one.

From Grand Central, the 'local' kerwalloped across town towards the North River, crossing a huge brick viaduct that stretched across the empty flats of Harlem and then turning north along the river bank at the mouth of Spuyten Duyvil Creek.

'It means 'in spite of the devil'.' Petrosino explained.

Flynn didn't tell him he knew all about the legend of Antony van Corlear, bound on an errand for his master, Peter Stuyvesant, who'd come to the banks of the creek one stormy night and vowed he'd swim the torrent '*en spyt den duivel!*' In he went, and an eyewitness later testified that the brash Anthony had been seized by the leg by the demon he'd so rashly irritated, and dragged under, never to appear again.

Across the broad reach of the Hudson,

Flynn could see the craggy face of the imposing Palisades. Paddle steamers chugged across the rolling river, fishing boats rocking in their wake.

Thanks to Petrosino's advance calls, a room had been set aside for them to interview Giuseppe di Primo, so they didn't have to use the echoing visiting hall with its unpainted stone walls and the chairs on both sides of a long mahogany counter divided by a heavy wire mesh which prevented any prisoner touching, or being touched by, any visitor. The room the Warden set aside for them wasn't exactly a parlour in the Astor House, either; but at least it had a table, chairs, a window. Two guards brought Di Primo in and sat him down. One of them remained by the door, inside the room, his face so studiously uninterested that it was plain he was listening carefully to everything which was said. Di Primo was perhaps forty years of age, although the baggy, striped prison uniform he was wearing made him look even older. His face was pasty white and drawn, and there were bluish shadows beneath his dark eyes. His hands were workworn and stained, fingernails broken and blackened from picking oakum. He kept his face absolutely without expression as Petrosino invited him to sit down.

'I'm Lieutenant Petrosino, New York Police Department, Di Primo,' the detective said. 'Like to ask you some questions.'

'Sure,' Di Primo said. There was a sneer in his voice. 'What else do cops do but ask questions?' His eyes moved over slowly to measure Flynn, contempt plain in them. 'You a cop too?'

'Sort of,' Flynn said. He just looked at Di Primo, keeping his eyes on the prisoner's eyes until Di Primo's gaze fell. For some obscure reason it made Flynn feel better.

'*Preferisce parlare in Italiano?*' Petrosino asked.

'No, I wouldn't,' Di Primo snapped. 'Talk English.'

'All right,' Petrosino said. He waited a long moment before speaking, as if knowing that by doing so he could bring back the wary apprehension in Di Primo's eyes.

'Where you from, Giuseppe?' he said finally. 'You born here or in the Old Country?'

'Napoli,' Di Primo said, chin rising a little, proudly. 'Barra.'

'Ah,' Petrosino said. He looked at Flynn and nodded meaningly. Flynn didn't know what the hell Petrosino was up to, but he wasn't about to let Di Primo know that. He nodded back as meaningly as Petrosino.

'What's that?' Di Primo said, faint alarm in his tone. 'What's with the 'ah' business?'

'Nothing,' Petrosino said.

'Skip it,' Flynn added.

'I say I'm born in Barra, you make it sound like something special. You give each other the eye. What the hell does that mean?'

'It doesn't mean a thing, Giuseppe,' Flynn said.

'But it might explain something,' Petrosino added, lips pursed.

'Explain what? What's to explain, for

Chrissake?' Di Primo snapped. 'You got a cigarette?'

'Sure,' Flynn said, tossing a pack on to the table. 'Help yourself.' Di Primo inhaled the smoke greedily, tucking the pack into the breast pocket of his uniform with an almost furtive haste. His eyes shuttled from Petrosino to Flynn, back again, and back again.

'You guys want to tell me what the hell you're getting at?' he said.

Petrosino looked at him in surprise, his eyebrows rising. He lifted his shoulders, spread his hands in a slow, elaborate shrug.

'We're not getting at anything, Giuseppe,' he said mildly. 'We just wondered how you came to take the rap for that counterfeiting case in Pittsburgh.'

'What you talking about?' Di Primo said. 'What is this, anyway?' His voice was aggrieved, as if Petrosino was picking on him unfairly.

'Just struck me as funny,' Petrosino said. 'There were five of you running that operation, right? Five Italians.'

Di Primo's eyes narrowed, and there

was rat cunning behind them. 'Yeah,' he said. 'An' six Germans, four Russians, an' two Chinese.'

'Come on, Giuseppe,' Flynn said. 'You know what we're getting at.' He hoped to God Di Primo did, or Petrosino did. *He* sure as hell didn't.

'You know it all,' Di Primo said. 'Why you askin' me?' There was a thin trace of apprehension in his voice, no stronger than a baby's sigh, but both the listening men heard it. Go get him, Joe, Flynn thought.

'They set you up, Giuseppe,' Petrosino said.

'Sure,' sneered Di Primo. But he was uneasy.

'Four of you went down,' Petrosino insisted. 'The one that got away, though, the engraver — he didn't take a fall, did he, Giuseppe?'

'What engraver?' Di Primo said. 'What the hell you gassin' about, copper?'

'You're from Barra, right?' Petrosino said. His change of tack bothered Di Primo enough to bring his head up, puzzlement on his face.

'Yeah, I'm from Barra. I told you already.'

'And the other three?'

'I don't get you.'

'Where they from, Giuseppe? Naples? Salerno? Caserta?'

'You're nuts.'

'Sure. And the engraver — where was he from?'

'How the hell would I know?' snarled Di Primo.

'You'd know,' Petrosino said. 'Sicilian, right?'

Flynn got it now and played his hand like Petrosino. 'Funny all you Neapolitan boys were sent up for five to seven, Giuseppe,' he said, as if thinking aloud. 'Only you.'

'You're *pazzo*, copper!' Di Primo shouted. 'They wouldn't do that to me!'

'Oh?' Petrosino said, softly. 'You're something special, that it? You're a *capo* maybe. You're connected. That's why they're pulling strings to get you out of here, huh? You cheap punk, those Sicilians wouldn't give a shit if I told the Warden to throw the key of your cell away!'

'That's not true!' Di Primo shouted, banging the table with his fist in frustrated anger. '*Non e vero!*'

The guard at the door started forward, hand on his baton, but Petrosino waved him away, almost absently, pulling back his jacket to reveal the big Smith & Wesson .38 tucked into the waistband of his trousers. The warder nodded, reassured. Nobody was going to chew him out if Di Primo broke someone's arm. He saw himself telling the Warden, 'But what could I do, sir? They had a repeating pistol and they couldn't stop him.'

'It's true, all right, Giuseppe,' Flynn said. 'You've been left holding the bag. The Sicilians got away with the plates, the money you'd printed, everything.'

'Fat lot you know,' Di Primo said now.

'I've got some sources in the *quartiere*, Giuseppe,' Petrosino said. 'That's not what they tell me.'

'Stick 'em up your ass!' snapped Di Primo. 'I'm connected. They're looking after me. Someone's making sure of that.'

'Uhuh,' Petrosino said, reflectively. He slid a photograph out of the brown manilla envelope he'd taken from his document case while Di Primo was talking. He laid it on the table gently and then slid it across to where the prisoner could see it.

'You know this man, Giuseppe?' he asked.

Di Primo looked at him, and then at Flynn, as though expecting some sort of trap. The faces of both men were bland, expressionless.

'Sure,' Di Primo said eventually. 'That's Nitto. My brother-in-law.' He looked at them as much as to say, 'so what?'; and as he did, he saw the suppressed excitement in their eyes.

'What is this?' he said again. 'What the fuck is this?'

'What's his name, Giuseppe?' Petrosino asked.

'Who?'

'Nitto. Your brother-in-law.'

'What brother-in-law?'

'Come on, Giuseppe, you're being stupid.'

'If you say so,' Di Primo said. His face was flat, sullen.

Petrosino sighed and slid another picture out of the manilla envelope. This one showed the corpse in the barrel just exactly the way Peter Nash had seen it on the pavement down in the lower East Side. He flicked the picture on top of the first one and let Di Primo take a good look at it. It wasn't a pretty picture and it brought a deep, shocked, stunning fear into Di Primo's eyes. He looked like a professional disbeliever who's just seen a ghost. Nobody spoke.

'What's his name, Giuseppe?' Petrosino repeated gently.

'What?' Di Primo tore his gaze away from the photograph. His eyes crept gradually around until he was looking at it again. 'What did you say?'

'His name.'

'Madonnia,' Di Primo said. 'Benedetto Madonnia.'

'Why did they do that to him, Giuseppe?'

'Oh, no,' Di Primo said. 'Oh, no. No you don't, copper.'

'You know what that means, *genitale en la bocce*?' Petrosino persisted.

'I said enough already,' Di Primo said.

'Have your fun,' Petrosino said. 'While you can.'

Di Primo spat on the floor.

'Stop that!' snapped the guard at the door.

'Turn blue,' Di Primo muttered.

'You know what that means, Giuseppe,' Flynn put in, 'why they do that to someone.'

Di Primo said nothing. He just looked at the photograph. His eyes were empty and his mind somewhere a long way away.

'Let me make a guess at what I think's going on, Giuseppe,' Petrosino said. 'You want me to do that?'

Nothing.

'I thought you would,' Petrosino said. 'So I'll tell you. I think the Sicilians are getting together to put you Neapolitan *Camorristi* out of business. I've got a hunch they don't want to cut you in any more. They want it all. There's someone new at the top of the *alianza*, someone who's decided to shake out all the loudmouths like Madonnia. I think your brother-in-law shot off his mouth and that's why he wound up dead in an alley with his balls cut off. That's what I think. How about you?'

Di Primo lifted his head and just looked at Petrosino. He said nothing, but there was something behind his flat gaze, something that skittered and clawed like a trapped animal, worrying, gnawing, uneasy.

'Benedetto Madonnia,' Flynn said. 'What was he, from Naples too?'

'Tuscanny,' Di Primo said, sullenly.

'Ah,' Flynn said.

'There you go with that fuckin' 'ah' business again!' snapped Di Primo. 'What the hell are you trying to say, anyway, for Chrissake?'

'Only what we said before, Giuseppe,' Petrosino told him. 'Not a Sicilian, see?'

'Jerk off!' snapped Di Primo.

'Somebody must have fixed his wagon,' Petrosino said, undaunted by the venom in Di Primo's voice. 'You want to give us a name to work on?'

'Yeah, President Roosevelt,' Di Primo sneered.

'What happened, Giuseppe?' Flynn said. 'You think he asked for too much? Or threatened somebody who didn't like being threatened?'

Nothing. Flyn decided to throw a wild card in, see what happened.

'Was he in on the counterfeiting with you?'

Di Primo just looked at him, but again Flynn caught that unease behind the eyes. It was the first time he'd experienced *omerta*. He'd heard about it. Petrosino had explained it. Hitting it head-on was something else again.

'You want to save us some legwork, Giuseppe?' Petrosino said. 'Give us Madonnia's address?'

'I wouldn't piss on you if you was on fire,' Di Primo told him conversationally.

Flynn saw Petrosino stifle the anger that rose behind his eyes. For a count of three he wondered whether the detective would hit Di Primo, and then he saw Petrosino exert that iron control he had. He must get this all the time, Flynn thought. It must be rough sometimes.

'You've got a big mouth,' Petrosino

said. 'That'll make it all the easier for them to fix you the way they fixed Nitto.'

'I'd like to see them try it,' Di Primo said.

'You give us some names, maybe we can make sure they don't,' Petrosino said.

'Who d'you think it was. Lupo the Wolf, maybe?'

'Jesus, you're dumb!' Di Primo said disgustedly.

'Sure,' Flynn said. 'But *we're* walking out of here later.'

'One name would do, Giuseppe,' Petrosino said softly. 'One name. Someone we can talk to.'

'Shit!' Di Primo said. 'I wouldn't trust you to find your ass with both hands at high noon using a mirror. You know anything about our thing, you ought to know I'll be looking into this myself when I get out of here. Personal, like.'

'*If* you get out,' Petrosino corrected him, gently.

'What's that supposed to mean?'

'The *amici* have long arms, Giuseppe. They can get you as easy in here as on Hester Street.'

'Why would they want to do that?' Di Primo said, without thinking.

'You're right,' Petrosino said, getting up off the chair and nodding to the guard at the door. 'Why would they bother with a cheap little *picciotto* like you? Come on, Flynn. This bum hasn't got the sense to know when he's been screwed to the wall.'

Flynn nodded, shrugged, got up off his chair. Di Primo scrambled to his feet, hand outstretched as though to detain them. 'Hey,' he said. 'Wait a minute.'

Petrosino was already at the open door. He paused, as if reluctantly, and turned. Flynn stopped, too.

'What now?' Petrosino said, wearily.

Di Primo looked at both men for a moment, and then they saw the decision come into the dark eyes, hooding them.

'Nuthin',' Di Primo said. He stared at the concrete floor, hunching his shoulders as if it had suddenly become cold. Petrosino shrugged and then led the way out of the room into the corridor. The second guard, who'd been standing outside, went in, and he and his partner

151

marched Di Primo off to the right, back to the cells. Di Primo went along, shoulders still slumped, without looking back.

'*Omerta*,' Petrosino said. 'No way to fight it.'

They went down the stairs and into the Warden's office. Half an hour later they were in a paddy-wagon being taken down to the station, and soon afterwards clattering back towards the city in the train. Flynn nursed his own thoughts, going over and over the things Di Primo had said. There'd been something there, he knew. He hadn't got his fingers on it, but there was something. He looked at Petrosino. The detective looked worn, tired out.

'You believe all that stuff you were telling Di Primo about the Sicilians trying to cut out the Naples boys, Joe?' he asked.

'It's one theory,' Petrosino said, as though reluctant to discuss the matter at all.

'Why would they do that?' Flynn persisted. 'Start a war among themselves?'

'They do it.'

'Yes, but why? It doesn't make sense.'

'It does if you remember one thing.'

'What's that?'

'Sharks never share,' Petrosino said.

7

There was a light breeze coming in off the sea, just strong enough to make the flags and bunting all along the boardwalk snap and flutter above the heads of the crowds beneath. A steamboat was churning its way around Norton's Point, passengers crowding to the side to see the lighthouse and the fog bell. The beach was not too crowded, although there were plenty of people around, more than enough to have brought out the beach-vendors and the hustlers, the donkey-ride concessionaires, and the Punch and Judy man with his fibreboard suitcase. There were people gathered giggling over their tintypes outside the photographer's hut with its legend GREATEST FERROTYPE GALLERY ON EARTH! and lines of people waiting at food stalls serving meat pies and patties and clam chowder. There were people playing croquet on the lawn of the Oriental, up on the eastern end of the island at Manhattan Beach and having just as much fun as those who were attracted by the more plebeian variety shows and shooting galleries, and the restaurant built in the form of an elephant off to the western end of Brighton Beach. They said there was nothing on the Tenderloin you couldn't find in Coney Island, whereas no hotel in the midtown part of Manhattan could boast a twice-weekly firework display, as did the ornate wooden Manhattan Beach Hotel.

Ignazo Lupo liked Coney Island, always had, apart from the money he smelled here. Millions, he thought, it would be worth millions. All these concessionaires: they would need protection against vandalism, accidents, fights breaking out. All these food stalls: they wanted to be sure that hoodlums would not complain about the quality of their food so vehemently that it would end with the stall in ruins, all its crockery broken, food spilled on heedless sand or concrete. Then the restaurants, the hotels, to whom disturbances of any kind would be anathema, who would willingly pay a regular premium to be certain that stinkbombs, drunks, felons, and prostitutes, were kept out of their salons and waiting rooms. Everywhere he looked, Lupo the Wolf saw possibilities, plenty of possibilities, which made him enjoy Coney Island even more. He'd loved it ever since he was a kid, and they'd gone down to the Battery on a Sunday, Mama and Papa and all the kids, to catch the steamer to Coney Island, coming home late at night well after dark, Papa smelling of garlic and rough red wine, the kids all doped and sleepy from the sea air and the sunshine and the hours of freedom on the sand, all that space after the warrens of alleys between tenements in seething Little Italy.

'Nice, huh?' he said to Morello. His *consigliere*, pacing softly alongside Lupo, nodded. He was dressed in a light, oatmeal-coloured jacket and dark slacks, and looked smoothly handsome. Women turned eyes in his direction as they went by, even when they were on some other man's arm. He must get a lot, Lupo thought enviously. He must get plenty. Still, that was the time to get it, when you were young. By God, he'd had plenty himself in the old days. They'd used to call him 'the Wolf' for different reasons in those days. He smiled to himself, at peace with the world.

'Niccolo,' he said, clapping the younger man on the shoulder. 'Is a nice day, hey?'

'Sure is,' Morello said. He was wearing dark glasses and Lupo couldn't see his eyes. That was another thing they were doing now, the younger ones. Dark glasses. They all looked like blind men, for Godsake!

'Tell you what,' he said to Morello. 'I'll let you buy me something to eat.'

Morello's face showed a trace of surprise, as though Lupo had said something unexpected. Then he smiled. 'I was just going to suggest it,' he said. 'I know a nice little place on Ocean Avenue.'

'Good, good,' Lupo said. 'Let's go, let's go.' He was having a good time. Thoughts of all the money he'd be able to make when they moved in on the Neapolitans and kicked their asses out of Brooklyn and Coney Island — all of Long Island, come to that, Queens too; not that there was that much at stake besides a few truck farms and what fishing there still was up the coast.

They walked up the avenue and eventually came to a little *trattoria*.

'Trattoria Scarpato,' Lupo said, reading the sign. 'Is good here?'

'Terrific,' Morello said. 'They got seafood here like you wouldn't believe.'

'Lead me to it,' Lupo smiled. 'And I'll tell you if you're right. There ain't a man in the State of New York knows seafood better than Ignazo Lupo.'

'That's right,' Morello smiled. 'That's right.'

They chose a table rather than a booth, so that Lupo could see out of the window. He liked to watch people walking by on their way to the beach, the kids all expectant, dragging at their parents' hands and yelling them to come on, walk faster, come on, daddy! He left the ordering to Niccolo. Niccolo knew what he didn't like, and if Niccolo said the seafood was good, he believed it. The young ones today, they had it different to what things had been like when Lupo was young. They had different ways. Me, for instance, he thought, I hadn't never even been in a restaurant until I was twenty-five. Niccolo, he could go eat at Delmonico's and never bat an eyelid, order them fancy dishes in French, with the right wines. He shook his head: things were a lot different to the old days.

They had spaghetti with clams and Niccolo was right, as usual; it was superb. Lupo called for more, and more Bardolino to go with it. It was a rest day. You couldn't really call looking over the terrain work; it was too nice a day to work anyway.

'*Anche de vino!*' he called, pushing back his plate, stuffing the last of the bread, soaked in the sauce, into his mouth with greasy fingers.

'What now, Niccolo?' he smiled. 'What other delights?'

'You wait,' Morello smiled back. The older man nodded, drinking deeply from the wineglass. Then the waiters came in with the lobsters and brought them big white linen napkins and bowls of water to wash their fingers and long-tined forks and more bread and another bottle of the good wine.

Finally, at nearly three o'clock, Lupo the Wolf pushed the littered plates away from himself, and belched. He smiled, not apologetically, at his *consigliere*, and patted his belly.

'*Bene*,' he said. '*Benissimo*, Niccolo. Truly very fine. Very fine.'

Nicholas Morello leaned over to light Lupo's cigar. 'I'm glad you enjoyed it,' he said. 'How about a *strega*?'

'No, no, nothing more to drink,' Lupo smiled, 'or I'll be asleep all the way back to the city. No, some coffee, perhaps. Good and black. And a pack of cards, eh? A game of cards?'

'Why not?' Morello said. 'Why not?'

They played cards idly, not really caring which of them won. The owner of the restaurant sat in for a few hands, then got up and stretched.

'I think I take a walk,' he said. 'You want to join me, Don Ignazo?'

Lupo the Wolf thought about it for a moment, then slapped the standing man on the rump cheerfully, chortling, 'No, no, I couldn't walk ten yards after such a meal. *Vai, vai!*'

Scarpato grinned at the older man's praise, gave a sort of bobbing bow, and went out into the street. He glanced back through the window at Morello, and the *consigliere* nodded infinitesimally. Scarpato's face went stiff with apprehension, and he scurried away.

'Come on, Niccolo,' Lupo grumbled, mock-testily. 'Deal, deal.'

'You deal,' Morello told him. 'I got to go.'

Lupo nodded, not looking up as Morello crossed the restaurant towards the men's room at the rear. A door marked GENTS led into a small washroom in which there was a toilet cubicle, a urinal, and a small handbasin above which was a sad, off-silver mirror. To the right of the mirror was a towel on a wooden roller; it was dank and grubby. Morello turned on both taps and stood looking at himself in the mirror. He could see the doorway behind him. It had a metal hook on the centre panel upon which to hang coats. One of the screws was missing.

Lupo the Wolf looked up as the four men came off the street, mildly curious, but only mildly, that anyone would want to eat this late in the afternoon. The puzzlement was still on his face when the four men produced sawn-off shotguns and fired them simultaneously into Lupo's head and body. The effective range was about four feet and the force of the spreading shot lifted the tattered body of Ignazo Lupo out of the bentwood chair in which he had been sitting and smashed it against the far wall of the restaurant at a height of about five feet. Then Lupo crashed down on to a table, reducing it to kindling, the smoking ruin of his corpse sliding to the floor, leaving an awful, glutinous smear down the gaily papered wall. The four men turned and went out of the doorway. By the time Nicholas Morello came out of the men's room and warily into the restaurant, they were nowhere to be seen.

'Well?' said Flynn. 'What now?'

He tossed the *Tribune* with its glaring headlines on to Petrosino's desk, and stood waiting for a reaction. Some hopes. Petrosino rubbed his stubbled chin with the heel of one hand, and looked up at the younger man reflectively.

'Dog's delight,' he said.

'What?'

' 'Let dogs delight to bark and bite,' ' the Lieutenant quoted heavily. ' 'For God hath made them so.' Newspapers!'

He said the last word with the bitter emphasis of a man who wasn't enamoured of the Fourth Estate, and it surprised Flynn. Petrosino had used the Press as successfully as any politician when it suited his own purpose. You might even have been forgiven for thinking, as some people not a thousand miles from this office patently believed, that Petrosino's newspaper coverage had been in great part responsible for his present rank of lieutenant. So his reaction was unexpected; it was the reaction of

163

someone who knows you can trust most newspapermen about as far as the door, and frankly Flynn was glad to see it. Working with saints has its drawbacks.

The boys at Printing House Square had gone to town on Lupo the Wolf's gory death. The *Tribune's* masthead was dwarfed by the two inch caps of the headline that screamed GANG LEADER SLAIN IN CONEY EATERY! In letters only slightly smaller, the reader's appetite was whetted with sub-heads that march across the whole front page shouting IGNAZO THE WOLF LUPO BLASTED! ON-THE-SPOT ACCOUNTS FROM OUR REPORTERS! HAPPENED IN THE BLINK OF AN EYE, SAYS LUPO'S FRIEND NICHOLAS MORELLO! LUPO LIKED CLAMS, SAYS RESTAURANT OWNER! ARREST IMMINENT, SAY POLICE! And so on.

In the close-packed columns of body-type below this nonsense, they raked over the usual morgue trash about the Black Hand and other 'secret societies', rehashed their hyperbolic hot air about the anarchists and the bomb throwers and the assassins who, leagued together, were bringing down the Republic from within. There were the usual cries for speedier action by the police in ridding the community of this, that, and the other menace, and po-faced editorials on the inability of the law-enforcement agencies to combat organized crime. And so on.

Everybody at Mulberry Street, everybody at City Hall, everybody in Greater New York, come to that, had seen them all before. The fact that the stories were misinformed was irrelevant. The fact that they compounded misinformation with even more misinformation was equally unimportant. The reaction was pretty much the same every time. An upsurge of ersatz outrage; a ringing speech or a prepared statement (those were Flynn's favourites) from the Mayor, promising immediate action; a clean-up campaign; an all-out attack on Department corruption; vows to lay the culprits by the heels. And so on.

This in turn would lead to a nominal or ritual kick in the ass for the Chief of Police, who would in turn issue a prepared statement or make a speech promising speedy retribution for all criminals within a radius of two thousand miles; details of present police strength; pleas for assistance from the public at large; the utterance of a number of highly charged and almost unreadable memos to captains of precincts and their patrolmen. And so on.

Then everything would slowly get back to normal, and the police would get on with the job they did as well as anyone could do anything in Manhattan. They didn't complain because there was roughly only one uniformed officer for every four thousand people on the island. They didn't complain — well, not much and not in public — about the dilapidated equipment and the lousy communications machinery and the tortuous chain of command and the ass-kickers and the freeloaders and the graft-takers and the time-servers. Not much, although some. They just got out on the streets and on with the job. What else were you going to do?

'Have we got anything?' Flynn asked.

'Not much,' Petrosino shrugged.

He explained that — information in the newspapers to the contrary — there'd been nothing at the scene of the murder which was going to help them. He dug into the pile of papers on the right-hand side of his desk and pulled out several of them.

'Here's the report of the patrolmen who were first on the scene,' he said.

'The police surgeon's report of his examination of the body. DOA report from the coroner's office. Murder Squad report. Detective's reports on interviews with Nicholas Morello and the restaurant owner, Scarpato.'

'And?'

'Nothing,' Petrosino said heavily. 'Like I said, nothing. Morello didn't see anything or hear anything except the shots. Scarpato the same. The three monkeys have got nothing on these boys.'

'How about the medical report?'

'Four shotguns fired into Lupo at a range between three and six feet,' Petrosino said. 'I imagine you don't want the details?' There was a wry smile on his face as he said it.

'Four shotguns, yet nobody heard anything or saw anything?' Flynn said.

'Oh, everybody heard something,' said Petrosino. 'Maybe some people even saw something. Men running out of the place, maybe, carrying guns. But we've got about as much chance of getting them to say so as we have of flapping our arms and flying like birds.'

He picked up the *Tribune* and tossed it aside. 'Arrest imminent,' he sneered. 'Somebody downstairs must be consulting a fortune teller if he think's that's true.'

'So what do we do now?' Flynn asked.

'Start with the known facts,' Petrosino said. 'Proceed from there.'

'Okay,' Flynn said. 'We know Lupo was killed by four men with shotguns. We know Lupo was a *capofamiglia*. We know Morello is — sorry, was, his counsellor.'

'Which is what makes it all so interesting,' Petrosino mused. 'The shotgun killing is real Mafia speciality. In Sicily, they call the shotgun the *lupara*. It's almost a ritual killing weapon, an execution weapon.'

'So we assume an execution?'

'I think so, yes. Morello's convenient trip to the washroom suggests he was in on it, knew what was coming.'

'Maybe even arranged it?'

'It's possible.'

'So we pick up Morello?'

'No,' Petrosino said. 'That would be a waste of time. We'd never get a word out of Morello, and someone would be in the Tombs so fast with a writ of habeas corpus to spring him it would make your head spin. No, let Morello be for the moment. Maybe we'll put someone on his tail. Let's see.'

'Okay, we've got an execution,' Flynn said. 'Why? Why would they knock off one of their top people?'

'Good question,' Petrosino said.

'Well, you're the expert,' Flynn riposted. 'Answer it.'

'No can do,' Petrosino said. 'But I know a couple of people who might be able to. Come on, get your hat.'

He took his own derby off the hatstand and swung the door back, heading out into the corridor before Flynn had properly grasped that Petrosino was actually going out. Snatching his own hat off the hook, Flynn ran down the stone staircase, his footsteps echoing off the tiled walls, and caught the stocky detective on the landing below.

'Where the hell are we going now?' he panted.

'To the only place we can get the kind of information we need,' Petrosino told him, not slackening his pace, going on down the stone stairs two at a time. 'On the streets!'

8

Salvatore Pignaroza was strictly small-time. He lived in a cluttered one-room hovel on the first floor of a tenement building on Hester Street, and made what nickels and dimes he could from running errands for some of the slightly bigger-time thugs who were his neighbours, acquaintances, and social superiors. Since he didn't give a good wholesome goddamn where he got his bread from, Sal also made what he could from con tricks, badger games, panel thieving, running women, or even the picking of pockets. He wasn't what you'd call particular. Just so he had enough of the green, to eat when he was hungry, which was now and then, and drink when he was dry, which was pretty much all of the time.

In his palmier days, when he was in his twenties and just off the boat, his aquiline Sicilian good looks, coupled to a certain bucolic charm, had made it possible for him to live off a series of women. However, as the years went by, and more and more good-looking Italian boys poured off the boats, some of them considerably tougher than Sal would ever be, he progressed downwards in the class of woman who'd work for him, with a corresponding loss of income that Sal, whose tastes were if anything now rather more expensive than less, could scarcely sit still for. So he moved over to the con game.

Nothing big, of course.

Uptown, if you had the front and could dress the part, you might easily be able to pull off a really big-time job, one of those hundred thousand dollar touches you now and again heard about. Downtown things were a bit earthier. There were still plenty of shills rooking the rubes for the 'toll' to cross the Brooklyn Bridge, even one or two who still tried to sell it to some hayseed with straw in his hair. Those were throwbacks to the palmier days, however, and things had become a little more sophisticated by the time Sal got into the game. He did all right, though. He managed to convince enough of the newly arrived *paisans*, stumbling out of Castle Garden with everything they owned in a duffle-sack on their teenage kids' shoulders, that they were in a land where a *paisan* couldn't trust anyone except another *paisan*, and that if they didn't want to be mulcted out of their hard-earned savings before they'd got ten blocks uptown, they'd take his advice and think about investing in gold. Imagine bringing your life savings all the way from the Old Country, he would tell them, and then some smooth-talking con man sells you worthless stocks and bonds. *Poof*, your money's gone. Or some shill sells you a place to live, and you find out for maybe a week, two weeks, that the property is condemned, you're out on the street, no place to live and all your money gone. New York is a hard town for strangers, especially if they don't speak the lingo too good. Better you put your savings into gold. Gold is the standard by which they measure the dollar in the United States; gold is the foundation on which all the banks operate; gold opens the doors of the brokerage houses to you; gold is the passport to the counsel of investment counsellors; gold is the currency of the express offices. Of course, it was difficult to buy. Everyone wanted it, you understand. Now for a *paisan* just off the immigrant ship, he had to say that buying gold would be the next thing to impossible, but . . . well, something might be done. It was a good spiel. Usually, by the time he'd finished, Salvatore Pignaroza had them slavering at the mouth. If he'd told them it was up top of the nearest 'skyscraper' they'd probably have taken a running leap at trying to climb it barehanded.

So, to cut a long and sad tale short, Salvatore hooked them. He had some lead, bought off the street gangs who made their drinking money stripping it off the roofs of churches, in bars and strips of various sizes, nicely finished in matt gold paint of the kind they used to paint picture frames, and — for a consideration — he sold some of it to the marks. The details of price, and so on, aren't really all that important. What's important was that Salvatore relieved some illiterate *mandriano* of all his savings, which enabled Sal to play the big shot in the quarter for a couple of weeks. Buy the boys a drink, rub shoulders with some of the *amici*, get a small connection going, you know the sort of thing. And when the money was gone, Sal would spruce himself up in his nice black suit with the broad chalk stripes, put on a relatively clean white shirt, get his shoes shined, and head on down to the Castle Gardens to try his luck again. He was doing all right, Salvatore Pignaroza.

Until Petrosino.

One of Sal's marks had done the unthinkable: gone to the police. They'd burst into the vestibule of the Fourth Precinct, filling the place with shrill and hysterical demands in the Neapolitan dialect for revenge, and the return of their life savings, and anything else they could think of to shout at the tops of their voices. The desk sergeant, not recognizing more than two small pebbles out of the avalanche of words that was cascading upon his defenceless head, said the only thing he knew to stop it, the secret formula, the magic wand.

'Get Petrosino!' he said.

Joe calmed them down, listened to their story, got all the details. Their name was Renis. Virginio Renis and his wife Maria, with their three small children, two girls and a boy, come all the way across the ocean to find a job in the New World; he a mechanic, a good mechanic, willing to work; and what would they do now with all their hard-earned money gone, no money to eat, no place to sleep, the *bambini* worn out from tramping the streets. What kind of a place was this America, anyway, where an Italian preyed upon his own kind?

What could you tell them?

Petrosino had helped them, found them a place to stay — some friends of his cousin in Staten Island. He loaned them some money — his own, as it happened. And then, with a determination which had awed some of his fellow detectives, he had spent the next three weeks on the street looking for the man or men who had robbed the Renis family. Three weeks in which he didn't sleep much, didn't eat much; three weeks in which he more and more looked like a stubbled bum on the downhill slide. Except he did it. He did it, all right. He nailed Salvatore Pignaroza and hauled him into Mulberry Street and stood him on a bench beneath a bright light so that the Renis family could identify him, which they did with commendable promptitude. They had to take what satisfaction they could from the fact that Salvatore would pull a nice long stretch in Sing Sing, because there was no way to get back a dime of their money, long since blown to the winds in the dives and backstreet bars of the quarter. Sadder, perhaps wiser, the Renis family went its way with a somewhat understandably low opinion of the United States of America in general and New York in particular. They eventually settled in Milwaukee, and made good. In later years, Virginio Renis would often tell the story of how he lost his savings. It made him almost a celebrity.

Salvatore Pignaroza went up to Sing Sing, and when he'd served a year Joe Petrosino came to see him. Sal wasn't particularly delighted to see the man who'd sent him down, but he wasn't given any choice about whether he would or not. However, no son of a bitch in the world was going to make him talk to Petrosino, he vowed. So he sat mute on his stool behind the wire mesh, his face sullen and set. For a while, anyway. Petrosino explained certain things to him, very clearly, very persuasively. Told him what would happen if he decided to co-operate; what would happen if he decided not to. Told Salvatore to think them over and let him know.

Sal thought them over.

He weighed the fact that he was a Sicilian, brought up on the basic premise that you tell the law nothing, against the fact that two more years in the hole was a long time; and if Petrosino, the son of a bitch, put the fix in, it would be four more years. He weighed the fact that what the detective was asking might endanger his life, against the offer Petrosino had made of a regular ten dollars a week, with bonuses for any tip he could act on. He weighed the fact that, generally speaking, all he would be able to pass on would be street gossip, against what he knew the *amici* did to people who talked loosely about their affairs.

He told Petrosino to go to hell.

Ah, well, Petrosino sighed, getting up from his chair on the civilian side of the heavy wire screen, it was a pity. Not only was Sal going to serve his full stretch — Petrosino would see to that — but when he did come out, Petrosino was going to let it slip that he was a stoolie anyway. With the word out on the street that Sal was a fink, an informer, the effect would be exactly the same as if he truly was, right?

'You wouldn't,' Salvatore said, knowing how wrong he was.

'Try me,' Petrosino suggested.

So Salvatore Pignaroza decided to reconsider his perhaps hasty decision; and when he finally came out of prison, paroled for good behaviour after eighteen months more of the nominal two years still to be served, he was used as Petrosino used a series of ex-busts like Sal, scattered here and there throughout Manhattan and the Bronx and Brooklyn; mostly — but not all — Italians who could provide him with the word on his patch, the street gossip, what people, being people, could not resist saying to each other about the private lives of certain other people. It was the kind of information to which no policeman could ever be privy, and even if eighty per cent of it was just dirty washing, there was always the chance that someone somewhere would give him a hard fact he could follow up, a hook to hang some *mafioso* on. He'd got a special fund set up, not much, but enough to pay off his people when he wanted to. He reckoned it was well worth the dollars, and so far nobody had given him any trouble over it. He figured they probably regarded it as part of the price they had to pay to be able to hand over all the shittiest cases to 'the Dago'.

Petrosino explained this tersely to Flynn as they loped through the crowded streets of the quarter. Salvatore Pigna-roza's usual hangout was in a saloon, Nel Mondo Vecchio, not far from his grubby room on Hester Street.

'How many of these informers have you got, Joe?' Flynn asked, as they hurried along. He saw Petrosino's eyes hood; the Lieutenant was deciding whether to confide or not again, he thought.

'Maybe a dozen altogether,' Petrosino said. 'Four you could call full-time, if you take my meaning.'

Flynn took his meaning. Informers were a special breed of people and one of the things you had to be careful not to do was overwork them, ask them for information outside their sphere of experience. Being dependent on you for goodwill — and cash — they were inclined, like Red Indians asked about the Custer massacre, to provide you with the answers you seemed to want, inventing them where necessary. So you used most of your stoolies only when their specialist knowledge of an area or certain people was involved. He imagined the four 'full time' informants were all within the sprawl of Little Italy.

Nel Mondo Vecchio wasn't much of a saloon, even as saloons went down in the quarter. It was a drinking-place, one of those near bucket-shops where the proprietor had a deal going with the local cop so he wouldn't get busted or moved on. The bar was pine planking resting on three barrels. There were shelves on the wall behind it; tables and chairs, even some straight benches that looked as if they might have been bought — or stolen — from a school, scattered around the place. It was just one big basement room situated beneath a barber shop, and rented by the month from the *padrone* who owned the tenement.

It was very much a local joint. Here a man could get a glass of cheap wine, a *grappa*, for a few pennies, sit and talk with friends or neighbours who lived in the same rat-infested tenements as he did, who shared the same hardships, the same high prices, the same overcrowding. A man came to a place like this because there were maybe five, six kids, and his

182

wife, in their two-room apartment — just to get out for a while, change one foetid atmosphere for another. After anything up to twelve hours in a factory, maybe as many as sixteen hours if business was good, a man deserved at least a break, a game of dominoes with his cronies perhaps, or penny bets on a greasy deck of cards. *Stranieri* never came into a place like Nel Mondo Vecchio. Even people from a couple of blocks away weren't welcomed. The atmosphere would become freezingly unfriendly until they shuffled their feet, moved uncomfortably in their seats as though expecting physical attack, and finally slid out with their tails between their legs, to seek more congenial surroundings.

Thus all conversation ceased as though shut off with a switch when Joe Petrosino barged into Nel Mondo Vecchio, glowering at the frozen tableau of hostile faces from beneath lowering brows. In his derby hat and Prince Albert coat, Petrosino looked as out of place as a tarantula in an Impressionist painting, but although he glowered as well as the

183

next man, his frown was no match for some of the looks directed back at him. Flynn stood at Petrosino's right shoulder, his own face as forbidding as he could make it. The space between his shoulder blades felt curiously exposed. Imagination, his commonsense told him. Like hell, his instinct replied. He watched as Petrosino stalked across to the rough bar and banged a photograph on the planks. It was a picture of a man Flynn had never seen.

'I'm looking for this man,' Petrosino said to the owner of the place, a cadaverous-looking individual with long black sideburns and a thick-lipped, nervously twisting mouth.

'Never seen him,' the man said without looking at the picture.

'Name of Petacco,' Petrosino said. 'Veglio Petacco. Hangs around this part of the quarter a lot.'

'Never seen him,' the man behind the bar repeated. 'You a copper?'

'No, I'm Cinderella,' Petrosino said. 'You sure you've never seen this Pettaco?'

'Certain,' the bartender said. He

couldn't have looked more guilty if they'd caught him with a meat axe in his hand standing over a headless body. His eyes slid to meet Flynn's and Flynn glared at him. He didn't know what the hell this Petacco had to do with the case, if anything, but he wasn't about to let anyone in Nel Mondo Vecchio know it. Petrosino, meanwhile, was holding the picture in front of the faces of the men at the tables.

'Any of you ever seen this man?' he asked, again and again.

The most polite answer he got was a sullen shake of the head. Mostly he got a blank disinterest or contemptuous disdain. One man spat on Petrosino's shoes, but the detective seemed not to notice. After a while he straightened up and shrugged.

'Nothing here,' he said to Flynn. 'Let's go. *Buon' notte, signore.*'

The man who spat on Petrosino's shoes spat again, this time into the sawdust on the floor. Otherwise the response to the detective's polite farewell was a stony silence. The two men came up the stone steps and into the muggy warmth of Hester Street. Flynn took a deep and grateful breath of the dank street air which, even if heavily aromatic, was country-fresh compared to the poisoned ice of the room they had just quit.

'What the hell was all that a — ?' he began.

'Not now,' Petrosino interrupted him, shaking his head. He grabbed Flynn's arm and steered him across the street. Then they hurried on up Hester towards Chrystie Street, crossing and going into a gaudy place on the corner of the Bowery. It was one of those big, mirrored, curlicued-wood-and-mahogany-long-bar places. Someone was playing the piano very badly up at the far end on a sort of raised dais, and a group of half-drunk celebrants were harmonizing 'Sweet Adeline' in discordant barbershop style. The saloon was L-shaped, and turning left at the top end near the piano, Flynn followed Petrosino into a darker area of curtained booths. A bosomy waitress in a short skirt came over as they sat down in one of the empty booths, plastering a simpering smile on her face. She looked about thirty, but Flynn guessed that beneath the paint she wasn't much more than eighteen or nineteen. They ordered beer and she switched her hips hopefully as she went back to the bar. She stopped when she saw they weren't looking.

'All right,' Flynn said. 'Explain.'

Petrosino held up a hand: wait. Flynn let his breath out in a slow, not-quite-exasperated sigh. Maybe he was wrong in allowing Petrosino to assume implicit command. Maybe he was wrong to let him take the lead, make the running. Petrosino had more than a big enough opinion of his own superior knowledge and connexions as it was. Flynn shrugged mentally. What the hell! Petrosino maybe needed to feel he was in command, that when he got into something people said, 'Watch out, here comes Petrosino.' Flynn understood Petrosino's drive, his need for recognition, his almost laughable vanity. They had come out of a lot of hard work, and a lot of giving up things other people weren't prepared to do without. Maybe he felt entitled. Either way, it was a pain in the back end, but Flynn figured he could live with it. Whatever Petrosino was up to, he'd find out in due course. Maybe in the end it would be a doublecross, but if it was, it would be as easy to spot as a dinosaur at a picnic. He'd already decided that you'd better be a fatalist if you wanted to work with Joe Petrosino.

It couldn't have been more than ten minutes later that he spotted the man. People who are looking for someone always stand out in public places. It's to do with a craning of the neck, the way the head moves, the way the body rises on the balls of the feet now and then; and the man who came into the saloon was obviously looking for someone. Flynn catalogued his description almost automatically: medium height, black hair, brown eyes, weight about a hundred and fifty; clothing, a cheap suit with the sit to the lapels that told an experienced eye they were lined with cardboard. The man's shoes — shoes are always a give-away — were cheap, scuffed, but well-polished. His hands looked well-kept. His shirt was white enough, the tie not noisy. The man saw Petrosino and his head came off the search position. He slid into the booth, bringing with him an air of garlic and apprehension.

'Bill,' Petrosino said. 'Meet Salvatore Pignaroza. An acquiaintance.'

'Uhuh,' Flynn said, playing Petrosino's game.

Pignaroza nodded nervously, his eyes flickering over Flynn and assessing him, much as Flynn had previously checked over Pignaroza. The underworld has its own recognition signals. The way a man dressed, the way he walked, talked, held himself: all these told an experienced eye whether he was a somebody or a nobody, an *amico* or John Law.

'He okay?' Pignaroza asked Petrosino.

'He's okay,' Petrosino nodded. 'What's biting you, Sal? You look nervous.'

'You,' Pignaroza said, as the waitress brought his beer and smiled at him. The smile bounced off Sal like an airgun pellet off an elephant. The waitress sniffed and moved off. 'You,' Pignaroza repeated. 'What's this, coming into Alfonso's like, like a . . . '

'Bull in a china shop?' suggested Petrosino.

'*Si, veramente.* Bull.'

'Wanted to see you, Sal,' Petrosino grinned. 'And fast. I knew you'd get the message.'

'Eh,' Pignaroza said. It was the sound of a man forced to accept stupidity on the part of someone who ought to know better, the sound of a man making his own small protest against something he knows he has no hope of changing, the sound of a man expressing a disgust he is not permitted to express.

'Benedetto Madonnia,' Petrosino said.

Salvatore Pignaroza's eyebrows jumped upwards before he could get them under control, but he was pretty quick. In the blink of an eye, he had slapped a studiously blank expression on his face. Petrosino didn't appear to have noticed the facial slip, and Flynn frowned. He kept his mouth shut, however. So far, Petrosino's methods had been anything but his own. But there were several different ways to skin a cat.

'Nothing?' Petrosino asked. Pignaroza shook his head.

'Okay,' the detective said. He took a sip of his beer and his eyes just touched Flynn's. Flynn saw the message in them, and he almost grinned. Think what you liked about the Italian, he was a pleasure to watch in action sometimes.

'What's the word on the Lupo killing, Sal?' Petrosino's question was put almost idly and again Pignaroza was caught off balance. This time his eyes widened so much that he knew he couldn't pretend to ignorance. He looked hastily around, as though expecting to find an assassin at his shoulder.

'Keep your voice down for Chrissake,' he muttered. 'You want to get me killed?'

'Not specially,' Petrosino said callously.

'Well take it easy, that's all,' Pignaroza muttered. 'That's dynamite.'

'Sure,' Petrosino said. 'Come on, Sal, I haven't got all night.'

'Listen,' Pignaroza said. 'I can only tell you what I heard, right?' His voice said that he wanted it made very clear that what he was about to tell them was not his responsibility and that if anyone asked them they were to be told that Sal

Pignaroza had only told them what he had heard, right? Flynn nodded, which seemed to reassure the Sicilian.

'Just tell us what you hear,' Petrosino prompted, gently.

'Well, the word is,' Pignaroza said, leaning forward across the table, his voice dropping to a conspiratorial level, 'the word is that Lupo wasn't holding his people together too good, and so they done the job on him.'

'You hear anything about who?'

'Hard to say that,' Pignaroza said, with his lower lip curling. 'You know, Loot. It don't pay to hazard that kind of guess.'

'Yeah,' Petrosino said. 'We heard it's maybe one of his own family. Nick Morello, maybe.'

'Jesus!' Pignaroza said, looking over his shoulder again. 'You crazy or something? I never said nothing like that. You can't say I did. I ain't going to say nothing like that, man!'

'Just trying it on for size,' Petrosino said, gently. 'Him having all that family trouble, like.'

'Hey, listen, don't tie me into nothing

like that,' Pignaroza said.

'Okay, Sal. What else you heard?'

'Street talk you mean?'

'Lupo the Wolf talk, I mean. Lupo got knocked off, remember? We just agreed it wasn't Nicky Morello that knocked him off. If it wasn't Morello, who was it?'

'Jesus, I don't know. I don't know. You think anyone'd tell me that?'

'I don't know what they'd tell you, Sal. What do they tell you?'

'Nothing, man. Nothing.'

'Nothing, huh? They just did the job on Lupo because they didn't like the way he ate clams, that it?'

'No, no, they . . . Shit, Lieutenant! This is only street gossip, you know. You couldn't put any faith in it.'

'Sure,' Petrosino said.

'The way I heard it, Lupo had some family trouble he couldn't handle. He was told to get it straight and didn't. So they hit him in the head.'

'Doesn't ring true, Sal,' Petrosino said. 'He was a *capofamiglia*, right?'

'Right, but — '

'Something else, Sal? You're very coy tonight.'

'Listen, Joe, what's it worth, if I give you something? Ten, maybe?'

'Let me hear it first.'

'Ought to be worth at least ten, Joe.'

'Try me and see.'

'Well, listen.' Pignaroza looked around, checking to make sure no one was watching him. Satisfied that nobody was, he leaned on the table again, his voice pitched low. 'Lupo had someone passing queer that wouldn't stop when the word came down from the top. He was told to get it organized or else. That's what I heard. On the street, you understand. Nothing to do with me.'

'Of course not,' Petrosino said softly. 'You think the Madonnia killing was connected, then?'

'Could be,' Pignaroza mused. 'I heard — ' He stopped abruptly and looked at Petrosino. 'You bastard!' he whispered.

'Ain't it the truth,' jeered Petrosino, mocking him.

Pignaroza drew in a breath and started

to curse. He kept his voice pitched low, but the venom was 100° proof. Without really changing his tone, eyes downcast and blazing, he called Petrosino every vile thing he could think of, and a good few he invented on the spot. Throughout the hissed tirade the detective said nothing, watched Pignaroza with almost reptilian equanimity. Finally, the Sicilian ran out of breath and stopped.

'All through?' Petrosino said, then.

Pignaroza started again, but this time his heart wasn't really in it, and after a moment or two, as if losing patience slightly, Petrosino reached across the table and put his hand on the Sicilian's forearm. He didn't appear to exert any pressure, but he must have done, for Flynn saw the other man's head come up sharply, saw the whiteness of pain bleach the skin below Pignaroza's eyes.

'That's enough, Sal,' Petrosino said, and there was flat anger in his voice. 'Now spill the rest of it, or I'll feed you to the rats on Mulberry Street.'

Pignaroza knew which rats he was talking about. The tension went out of his shouders and he slumped back in the seat. He nodded.

'Waitress!' Petrosino said, louder than usual. The girl came across. She didn't smile this time. Smiles were too valuable to throw away.

'Let's have some more beers here,' the detective said.

'Sure, honey,' she said automatically and went to get the drinks.

They sat there for nearly thirty minutes listening to Pignaroza's droning monotone. He told them all the street talk, because the street talk, and the pool-hall talk, and the saloon talk, and the brothel pillow-talk, were really all he knew. He told them that Benedetto Madonnia had been a *pezzonovanta*, a loudmouthed bigshot who'd spat in the eye of his own *capofamiglia*, which was, as everyone knew, why he'd wound up in a barrel with his balls cut off. As for Lupo, since he'd taken the problem upstairs, he'd been required to do certain things as back-up. What they were nobody knew, nobody was likely to find out, and come to that, nobody wanted to know — since whatever they were, the lack of doing them had probably resulted in Lupo's being shot to tatters in the Ocean Avenue restaurant of Vincenzo Scarpato. It was understood, although not spoken of, that Nicholas Morello had fingered his own *capo*, and this was considered to be an *infamità* by some of the older people in the *alianza*. Nobody was going to walk up to him and say so, of course.

Salvatore Pignaroza told the two men all this, and much more. The floodgates of his fear of the *amici* breached, he told them who was leaning on whom for a few extra bucks, who was in hock to the Jews for how much, who was taking a nice percentage off the traders on this street and that — and what he was doing with the money — and which ward-heeler was trying to muscle in on whose bailiwick. Little of what he told them was relevant to their main interest, but neither man interrupted Pignaroza. When you're panning for gold, you sure as hell don't dam the river. Oh, a lot of it was stuff that no intelligent patrolman would have bothered to investigate, much less report.

There was always petty crime on the streets and it was easier to watch it, note where it led, than suppress it. Besides, if you put the arm on every man who hustled a few bucks on the streets of Little Italy, you'd fill the already overflowing Tombs ten times over and still only make a slight dent in the crime rate. So they let Pignaroza ramble on until he was through, until he started to falter, until they could see him wondering whether to start inventing or embroidering. When that point came, Petrosino's eyes met Flynn's and he nodded.

'With Lupo dead,' Flynn said, picking up his cue, 'what happens now?'

'Well, Nich Morello takes over the East Side, I guess,' Pignaroza said, surprised to have to state the obvious.

'No,' Petrosino said. 'He means, who's the new man of respect, Sal? we hear a lot about him. A fixer, we hear. Very big. In charge of everything. That true?'

'Jesus, Joe!' Pignaroza said. 'Don't you go messing with him.'

'That big, huh?'

'That big,' Pignaroza said.

'The name?'

Salvatore Pignaroza looked around him edgily, licking his lips. Then he looked at the twenty dollar bill Petrosino was laying on the table, smoothing out the flat with the tips of his fingers.

'Twenty-five?' he said, without much hope in his voice.

'The name,' Petrosino repeated.

Pignaroza told him.

'Vito Cascio Ferro,' Petrosino mused.

'Quietly, for Chrissake!' hissed Pignaroza.

'Here's your twenty,' Petrosino said. 'On your way.'

Like a snake, Pignaroza's hand flickered out and palmed the bill. He got to his feet and nodded at Flynn. He extended his hand to Petrosino, who affected not to see it.

'See you again, Sal,' he said. It was brutal, but Flynn knew it was the way to handle the situation. You kept your informers at a good arm's length. They were not your friend. They weren't anybody's friend, because if they'd sell information to you, it had to figure they'd sell you to the next guy with a twenty dollar bill to waste. Pignaroza slouched off and Flynn looked expectantly at Petrosino.

'So,' he said.

'So, indeed,' Petrosino said. 'Now, my young friend: what do you think?'

'True, as far as he knows the difference between truth and lies,' Flynn judged. 'I don't think he's smart enough to make up a yarn like that.'

'No,' Petrosino agreed. 'However, he's dumb enough to try to set us up if someone told him he'd better do it.'

Flynn looked at Petrosino for a long moment before he spoke. Did Petrosino really think his enemies were as Machiavellian as that, or was it that he was so self-inflated that he believed he was important enough for them to go to that kind of trouble?

'How set us up?' he managed.

'Make us go after Ferro and make fools of ourselves,' Petrosino said. 'Well, we don't fall that easily. I'm going to talk to another guy I know.'

'That figures,' Flynn said resignedly.

'More legwork, right?'

'Oh, it's only a dozen blocks down-town,' Petrosino said. 'That won't kill you.'

'Sure,' Flynn said. 'Do I get to finish the beer?'

'All right,' Petrosino said. 'But hurry up, will you?'

He doesn't mean it to be offensive, Flynn told himself yet again. He really doesn't mean it. It just comes out that way. He drained his glass.

It had, of course, not occurred to either of them to watch Salvatore Pignaroza leave the saloon and consequently, neither of them had seen an unobtrusive-looking fellow in workman's clothes leave the booth diagonally opposite them and go out close behind Pignaroza. Equally, it did not occur to either of them that the second man in the booth would finish his drink rapidly as Flynn and Petrosino got up and walked to the door, or that he would follow them with the skill of a professional as they went downtown to find Giovanni Abruzzo, Petrosino's other stool-pigeon.

9

Don Vito brought peace.

He did it by removing the need for war, by a series of careful and brilliant conciliatory moves, by a number of neatly planned manoeuvres with which no individual *capofamiglia* could quarrel, and yet which effectively, in the end, stifled the growing tension between the *Camorristi* and the Sicilians. He drew up new territories in consultation with the heads of each family concerned, forbidding invasion in any fashion of the territory of one family by the soldiers of another. Brooklyn, all of it, handed over to the astonished but delighted *Camorristi* of Don Pelligrino Morano. The East Side, Lupo the Wolf's former territory, was now under control of Lupo's former *consigliere*, Nicholas Morello, and all the families agreed that Don Vito had been absolutely right in removing Lupo after his failure to produce incriminating documents which Madonnia had threatened to use. They had, of course, been recovered; nobody had connected the death of a cheap shyster on the East Side who'd been holding Madonnia's papers with the 'man in the barrel' case. So that was done, although Don Vito knew that eventually he or his successor would have to take action over Morello: a *consigliere* who agreed to betray his own *capo* could not remain long in a seat of power. Then Don Vito moved the rest of his chessmen. The West Side was to be run by Giuseppe Morello, Nicholas' brother. Then, the master-stroke: Giuseppe Fontana at the head of the Long Island family, which also covered Queens, and Giuseppe Masseria to control the Bronx. Let Don Pelligrino Morano and his *Camorristi* make one overt move towards war now, and the nutcracker of the Sicilian families surrounding him would close, devastatingly.

That it was little more than an agreed stalemate Don Vito knew. That it merely postponed a conflict which was, historically, inevitable he was equally aware.

Patchwork, he smiled to Antonio Lombrado, but effective for all its ragged edges. It would give his plan time to mature, give them all time to consider that the ideal which he had suggested to them was not some unattainable dream, but a realizable certainty. The *alianza* needed time, a time of peace in which the younger ones Don Vito had met now could grow. In fifteen years or twenty, if his work lasted long enough, they would be ready; strong and hungry. He ticked them off in his mind: Morello's *consigliere* Maranzano, here on the West Side in Manhattan; that slim youngster from Lercara Friddi, Salvatore Lucania; the two Mangano boys, Philip and Vincente. Vito Genovese was another. They would be strong and ruthless when the time came, and they would change the *alianza* to what the times demanded. If there was peace in the meantime.

So what was important now was that nothing happened to disturb the fragile calm. He sent word to everyone, and because of the enormous respect his achievements in Manhattan had engendered, his word was as law to most: there were to be no incidents. No confrontations with officialdom of any kind. It would be henceforth against the rules to attack, wound, or kill any police officer, any Federal investigator, any law-enforcement agent, without a full meeting of the council having approved the action. It was also forbidden to try to interfere with any newspaper reporter using either force or bribery, which might lead to publicity in the Press. Don Vito had other plans for the Press. There was now to be a determined effort on the part of everyone to use the power of the *alianza* politically. Concerted waves of letters from Italian immigrants in all walks of life — genuine immigrants, genuine letters; no coercion, just suggestion — would be sent to the Press, and to all kinds of politicians, from the President down to local labour leaders. These letters would all be different, of course, but their total effect would be to create a massive protest against the identification of solid working-class Italian citizens with the gangsters who infested the major cities.

There would be Italian parades, Italian street parties, Italian protest marches, Italian rallies designed to publicize the Italian as a good citizen, and also, of course, designed to make any newspaperman or politician wary of attributing any crime to Italian gangsters, secret societies or, when nearer the truth, *mafiosi*. Politicians no less than newspapers were impressed by numbers, especially when those numbers were organized and could cast votes.

All these activities, and many others, would, of course, be supervised by the *amici* themselves, and it was a tribute to Don Vito's astonishing presence, tact, and the respect in which he was held, that none of the families realized that he was keeping them so busy that they had little or no time to plot internecine war, vengeance, or murder.

Don Vito sent word of his plans and his progress to the other families, across the country in Pittsburgh, and Chicago, and New Orleans, and elsewhere. There were many expressions of admiration of his achievements, many warm messages of sympathy, love, and support, many examples of emulation, many letters signed *vi bacio le mani*. It would have been an almost complete victory, a total vindication of Don Vito's ideas except for one man.

Petrosino.

Antonio Lombrado told Don Vito about Petrosino's activities, which he had learned about first-hand from their contact in Police Headquarters at Mulberry Street, who had provided Lombrado with copies of Petrosino's reports. These were admittedly guarded; however, it meant that they knew of the inquiries which had been made at every barrel-maker in the State of New York, inquiries which had resulted in the identification of the one in which the mutilated body of Benedetto Madonnia had been found. It meant that they knew that the records of the barrel factory showed that there were only two places in Manhattan to which that barrel could have been delivered: a German food store on Third Avenue, or a restaurant on Elizabeth Street — the

Stella d'Italia Restaurant.

Don Vito reproached himself for not having paid enough attention to this *villano riffato*, for having seen him as most of the *amici* saw him, a publicity-hungry detective who had latched on to the lowest rung of the ladder of their existence and built up a reputation by arresting small-time thieves, *picciotti*, whom he could claim — since who would say otherwise? — were important members of what he called the Mafia. Now this Petrosino was in possession of information which, if not dangerous, was uncomfortable. And Lombrado added the information about Petrosino's informants, who had been watched, just as Petrosino had been watched, ever since Lombrado had learned of the progress of the investigation.

It was nothing more than a loose end, a frayed binding. No one who had seen anything would speak of it, of that Lombrado was sure, and Don Vito was prepared to accept his certainty. A barrel, after all, was only a barrel. It had been put outside in an alley, perhaps. Someone had stolen it, perhaps. After all, they'd steal the trousers off your legs in some parts of Elizabeth Street, if you gave them half a chance. As for Madonnia, that too had been taken care of long since. Quietly spoken men had passed the time of day with shopkeepers and pushcart peddlers along Elizabeth Street, passing the word, letting what was required be known. That what had happened that night in the alley on Bleecker Street was a matter of some people who preferred it not to be talked about. It was, of course, understood that one could connect observance of certain people's wishes in this matter with one's own personal safety, so by the time the quietly spoken men had visited whom they wished to visit, there wasn't a man or woman who'd have tipped a word to the cops for a gold clock and a hundred dollar bonus. There on the street, where four men had held the screaming Madonnia while a fifth used the knife on him, nobody had seen a thing, nobody had heard a thing, nobody was going to say a thing. Lombrado was satisfied of that, and he told Don Vito he was. All eventualities were checked, all avenues closed.

Don Vito was relieved, for his own rule about mayhem against police officers would have looked pretty silly had he been the first one to run to the council and ask permission to remove one. It would have diminished his own respect, made him look weak, frightened. It was no time for that, and he was glad. If Petrosino persisted, then he would have to find a way to totally discredit the man, and he was just as pleased that he did not have to do it. For the moment at least, Petrosino was no threat. They had every action he might take covered.

Except the one Petrosino hit them with.

He asked for, and got, warrants for the arrest of Vito Cascio Ferro, Giuseppe Morello, Giuseppe Fontana, Antonio Lombrado, and Tommaso Petto, for the suspected murder of Benedetto Madonnia, on evidence provided by one Guiseppe di Primo, presently serving in the penitentiary at Sing Sing.

★ ★ ★

Paul le Barbier was one of the few Manhattan lawyers who could afford to live on Fifth Avenue. To qualify that statement, it should be understood that it wasn't difficult to live on Fifth Avenue, providing you were talking about Fifth Avenue below, say, 23rd Street. It wasn't even hard to live on Fifth Avenue below 42nd Street because then you'd be living in the Tenderloin, and anybody who lived in the Tenderloin was, well, somebody who'd live in the Tenderloin, so to speak. However, above 42nd Street you were in a different world, and the further uptown past there you went, the more different it became, and the fatter your bank-roll had to be. Up at the top end of the Avenue were the mansions of the real rich, the ones who simply didn't know the size of their bankroll: the Rockefellers and the Vanderbilts and the Goulds, the merchant princes like A T Stewart, the newspaper kings like Hearst and Pulitzer, or even the merely vulgar like 'Diamond Jim' Brady. Here lived the Wall Street financiers and the industrial magnates, the sub-stratum of the Four Hundred who were in turn a sub-stratum of the Upper Tendom. Below the Goulds and Rockefellers and Stewarts lived the ones who drank at the Hoffman House and dined at Rector's, that astonishing palace of Lucullus where the head waiter was reputed to make tips totalling more than twenty thousand dollars every year, and where the coat-room boy *paid* the restaurant five thousand smackeroos a year for his concession.

You had to have plenty of the ready to live on that stretch of Fifth Avenue, and, well, if you want to know the truth, Paul le Barbier had more than plenty. He was probably one of the most successful criminal lawyers in the city, and if perhaps eighty or ninety per cent of his cases came from the area south of 14th Street which upmarket newspapers were now calling 'the melting pot', *tant pis*. No one in his wide spectrum of Society acquaintances thought anything less of him because his clients came out of that sprawling, spreading *mélange* of nationalities and identities pulsing and throbbing in a part of New York that few of them had ever seen or would ever care to see. No, if anything, Paul le Barbier was highly thought of because he seemed to care for the starving poor, who thronged unceasingly to the offices on Canal Street where le Barbier kept seven clerks to cope with the unending flow of work which came through their doors. It was a flow made no less great by the reputation of Paul le Barbier, of whom it was said that his clients only rarely, if ever, went to prison, and that if they did, it was because le Barbier could not get the Blessed Virgin to come and attest to their innocence. Bail bondsmen loitered close to the offices, solicitors, legal advisers, attorneys and charlatans — if you could tell one from the other — anyone finding himself with a client against whom the United States of America seemed to have an unassailable case, could and did send a messenger fleeting across Center Street and — if the need was great and the fee substantial enough — be sure that a phone call would be made and that shortly afterwards Le Barbier would be stepping out of his carriage, immaculately dressed and looking like the million dollars people said he had, to work his miracles in the courtroom.

What very few people were aware of was that Paul le Barbier was also the legal adviser of Don Vito Cascio Ferro, a position to which he had succeeded naturally upon the death of his earlier client, Don Gabriele Pantucci. Those very few people who did know knew also that Paul le Barbier had been born Paulo Barbiere some forty years before in the little Sicilian fishing town of Céfalu, eastwards along the coast from Palermo. Brought to the United States as a boy, he had been taken under the wing of his godfather, Don Gabriele, who had seen to it that the boy had a real education, the kind that only money can buy. So Paulo had received the very, very, best there was, graduating eventually from Columbia Law School *summa cum laude*, learning his business with the highly respected law firm of Ugast, Hart and

Schwartz. Long before this, of course, he had legally changed his name to Paul le Barbier, and had told the story of his French birth and upbringing so often that he all but believed it himself.

Don Gabriele had asked nothing of his protégé in those early years, content to sit back and watch the boy's skills grow, his experience deepen, his mastery of the complexities of his profession increase; watch him earn the respect of his peers. Meanwhile his home was always open to the young man, his advice always available and sometimes — not often, but when it was needed — his influence. Seats, perhaps, at the Opera on the right night. Tickets, maybe, to the Beaux Arts Ball. A reservation for a table at the Waldorf when no tables could be expected to be available. When these occasions arose, and they were seldom, then someone would make a quiet telephone call and what was needed was arranged.

Gradually Don Gabriele had brought Paul into his affairs. The transfer of a deed, perhaps, the making of a will, or the settlement of a probate for someone who had come to him for help from the *quartiere*. For such work, he had explained, there could be no fee, although Paul would be paid in other ways, at another time. These cases, and there were many — although never so many as to embarrass the young man in his early days — Don Gabriele referred to Paul le Barbier Associates as unthinkingly as he referred certain other problems to Antonio Lombrado. He received their accession to his wishes without thought of gratitude. He was all the 'Associates' Paul le Barbier would ever need or ever have, although it was a number of years before that happened. It did happen though. Gradually, perhaps; but inevitably. There would be a special case, a favour for a friend of the family. Then another, and another. Until Don Gabriele was sure that they all knew Paul and all trusted him as *un amico dei amici*. A friend. Of recognized and vital skills and great ability. The word was spread, without excitement, without haste. He's all right. Treat him with respect, he's okay.

So he was treated, and on top of that with the respect that a brilliant lawyer deserves, even if he was sometimes too American by half for some of the people he represented; even if he was too Fancy-Dan by more than half for some others, who resented his camel-hair coats and his large cigars, his hair that smelled of bay rum and his body that reeked of expensive cologne, because they were alien to their experience. What he did for them in court was something else, however, for he rarely failed, and in the ultimate analysis that was how they judged a man. Whether he was defending some obscure *picciotto* caught while doing his *capo's* bidding, or some hired *sicario* brought in from another city to do the job on somebody, or — as in one or two cases — patently guilty men, le Barbier came through, delivered.

In such cases, of course, he had a great advantage denied the public prosecutor. As defence counsel, he had the constitutional right to see the records and documents and testimony upon which the State was basing its case and to know of any witness whose appearance might help to convict his client. Paul le Barbier was great believer in constitutional rights and he exercised them on every possible occasion, despite not-so-veiled hints from many bested Assistant District Attorneys and such, that he passed that information along to certain other parties. They never said such things any place le Barbier might have heard them because they knew he would have sued the pants off them for slander: he had never been, and demonstrably had no need to be, involved in frightening off witnesses or issuing warnings of impeding personal catastrophe to jurymen. That he discussed the cases he defended with his partners he openly admitted. Whatever else happened was not his concern but the concern of the law-enforcement agencies of the City of New York. He neither advertised nor concealed. And if it bothered him that he spent the majority of his waking hours subverting the course of justice, no trace of remorse had ever been seen on his smoothly-shaven plumply pink face.

The news, therefore, that Don Vito

Cascio Ferro had been arrested was, when it was relayed to him at the elegant dinner party in a beautiful house overlooking the Hudson at Riverside Drive, appalling. He did not, could not, believe it at first. When he had been assured by his clerks that it was so, he made elegiacally formal apologies to his beautiful hostess and her equally beautiful husband for the fact that lawyers, like doctors and priests, may never call their time their own. He returned post-haste to his own home, and started to make telephone calls.

Within ten minutes he knew that the warrants had been issued to a Lieutenant Joseph Petrosino of the Police Department's Italian Branch based at the Mulberry Street building, and that the prisoners had been taken to the night court at the Tombs, where they would be arraigned before the judge the following morning. Within another ten minutes, one of le Barbier's clerks was dashing through the night in a cab to the home of Judge Albert Cardozo with a written request from le Barbier for five writs of habeas corpus in the names of Vito Cascio Ferro, Tommaso Petto, Antonio Lombrado, Giuseppe Morello, and Giuseppe Fontana. Judge Cardozo would understand, as he had understood many times before, that the following day, as soon as the banks were open, one thousand two hundred and fifty dollars would be delivered to him in a plain brown envelope — two hundred and fifty dollars for each writ and no questions asked.

Le Barbier's third call was to the Chief of Police, Michael O'Donovan, who, far from being annoyed at this unwarranted intrusion upon his privacy (he was eating dinner at his home on West 69th Street) scrambled out of the house, suspenders dangling, and made haste downtown the faster to discover the facts which Paul le Barbier had charged him with discovering — namely, the name or names of any witness or witnesses supportive to Petrosino's arrests, plus any other evidence written or otherwise which he might produce in court.

Within an hour of his having been informed of Don Vito's arrest, Paul le

Barbier presented himself at Police Headquarters and was ushered into the office of Chief Michael O'Donovan. There he learned that Petrosino's arrests had been made upon evidence provided by one Giuseppe di Primo, a convicted felon presently serving a three-year sentence at Ossining. Nodding graciously, his head wreathed in aromatic cigar smoke, Paul le Barbier laid the writs signed by Judge Cardozo on the Chief's desk. Softly, never letting any hint of a threatening tone enter his voice, le Barbier pointed out to the Chief what the Chief surely, he imagined, already knew. That the evidence of a convicted felon was not only specious but inadmissible, and that while he, le Barbier, was more than ready to watch the NYPD get deeper and ever deeper into the mire on this one, his personal regard for the Chief was so high that he was reluctant to see it happen. Surely the Chief knew that these men were highly respected Italian businessmen, thought of with the greatest esteem in the quarter? Hadn't he been reading his paper lately, hearing all about

221

the rallies and protest marches of the Italians-in-America League? Couldn't he imagine what those same newspapers would do when they got hold of a story like this, when they learned that one policeman with an obsession had arrested five Italian businessmen without the faintest shred of the kind of evidence which would stand up in court while he, Paul le Barbier, already had writs of habeas corpus which ensured their immediate release under any circumstances? Unless, of course, Petrosino had evidence other than that of a convicted counterfeiter.

Chief Michael O'Donovan winced even more sharply at this last than he'd been wincing all the way through Paul le Barbier's brutally beautiful outline of exactly what kind of mess Joe Petrosino had got them into now. He listened to the lawyer's silky suggestion that perhaps, all things being equal, it would be a great deal simpler to take the writs of habeas corpus down to the Tombs now, get a friendly judge in night court to set bail, and accept his, Paul le Barbier's solemn undertaking that none of those involved would fail to present himself should the case ever — much as he doubted that eventuality — ever come to court. Chief Michael O'Donovan knew when he was licked, and cursing the Petrosino family for generations past and generations to come, he placed a call to the Tombs.

Less than an hour later, le Barbier's clients were on the street, free on total bail of sixteen thousand dollars. Le Barbier personally guaranteed the sum, and when he was asked by the astonished judge how he could do so, replied airily that a collection would be made in the Italian quarter and that he had absolutely no doubt that he would be fully reimbursed.

10

'This it?' O'Donovan asked.

'That's it,' Petrosino said.

There was a silence in the room as the Chief of Police read the report Petrosino had handed to him. His lips moved as he read, a sibilant sub-mutter coming from his mouth. The report wasn't very long and it certainly wasn't very detailed. Joe Petrosino was giving no more away than he had to, and certainly no more than he had to give to Chief Michael O'Donovan, via whom, he was certain, his information would be passed on to the very people Petrosino was trying to convict. Even so, it was more than he had wanted to put on paper.

As soon as O'Donovan had demanded a full report on the arrest of Vito Ferro and the other four *mafiosi*, Petrosino had asked Bill Flynn to get up to Sing Sing as fast as he could and have a word with the Warden there, get him to take special precautions for the safety of Giuseppe di Primo. He hoped Flynn would be able to talk the Warden round, although it was doubtful anyone could. Special treatment for prisoners was not a speciality of the house at Ossining.

So he sat now and waited to hear what Chief O'Donovan thought of his report, as if he couldn't guess. Meanwhile his eyes moved restlessly, seeing this familiar room on the first floor of the six-storey Police Headquarters building as it had been when it had been Tom Byrnes' office. God, he thought, twenty years ago! At the far side of the room was a big window which looked out on to the bustle of Houston Street. One wall was lined with bookcases, floor to ceiling, although Chief O'Donovan used them more as decorative furniture — there were plaques and medallions and statuettes with which he'd been presented, in places of glory, at eye-level, while the books, which were just books, filled up the empty spaces he had no trophies to put in. In Inspector Tom Byrnes' day, they had been jammed with books on criminology, psychology, pathology, medicine, history, economics. But then was then and now was now. The glass-fronted cabinet which had housed Tom Byrnes' collection of old pistols was long gone, replaced by a roll-top desk cluttered with papers. As was the big claw-foot mahogany desk, scarred and burned along its edges by the forgotten cigars of a thousand vanished detectives. There'd been a drawing on the wall, Petrosino remembered: some yachts off Sandy Hook lighthouse. Now there were photographs of O'Donovan shaking hands with this politician or that stage personality. Many of them were signed. He was a real Sunday-outing of a Chief of Police, Michael O'Donovan was, Petrosino thought, as O'Donovan looked up from the report.

'You were going for a conviction on *this*?' the Chief asked, incredulously, tossing the report across the desk towards Petrosino.

'I was.'

O'Donovan shook his head. 'Joe,' he said, sadly. 'I'm beginning to get worried about you. This Italian secret society thing is — '

'Getting to be an obsession with me,' Petrosino interrupted. 'I know. That's what everyone tells me.'

'Joe,' O'Donovan explained patiently. 'Joe, you saw those people you hauled in. They weren't gangsters. They were goddamned Italian peasants. Jesus, they could hardly talk American!'

'Sure,' Petrosino said, sourly. 'And they whistled up the most expensive lawyer in Manhattan and sixteen thousand dollars in bail like goddamned Italian peasants, too.'

'That was le Barbier grandstanding and you know it,' O'Donovan said, the exasperation in his voice growing. 'You know he always takes on these cases out of the quarter and makes some kind of grandstand play. It's a kind of advertising for him, like some butcher giving an old lady a leg of lamb for ten cents once a week. It's good for business.'

'That part I believe,' Petrosino said.

'Joe, you know those goddamned Da — those Eyetalians down in the quarter. They're so honest down there, they'd break their backs before they left le

227

Barbier holding the bag on their default.'

'Or get them broken for them,' muttered Petrosino, not yielding an inch.

O'Donovan ignored the remark. He picked up the report and waved it. 'You never really thought you could make this stick, did you?'

'On the contrary,' Petrosino said.

'Joe, listen to me,' O'Donovan said, earnestly, 'I'm talking to you as a friend now, not Chief of Police. You couldn't even get the DA's office to prepare a case on this kind of evidence, much less go to court with it.'

'I got a warrant on it.' Petrosino said. 'Didn't I?'

O'Donovan slapped the report down on his desk with an exasperated sound. There was no point, as he ought to know by now, in arguing with Joe Petrosino. He knew better than any cop, better than the Chief, better than the Commissioners, the Mayor, the President of the United States, and no doubt Jesus Christ himself, if He happened to drop in and suggest Petrosino might be off track. Anger, like irony, like sarcasm, like scorn, like pity, all rolled off Petrosino without visible effect. Stubborn, mule-headed, short-sighted bastard, he thought. Every time three Dagos sit down at a table in some saloon, he figures it's a secret society planning to knock off the President again. Someone's got to put the mockers on him, and it might as well be me.

'Joe,' he said, sighing with theatrical heaviness, 'can you imagine what Paul le Barbier would do to us if we went to court with this di Primo as our chief witness? He'd take him to pieces in front of the jury and then take us for dessert.'

'I believe di Primo,' Petrosino said, flatly.

'Well ginger-peachy for you!' O'Donovan snapped, letting the building anger burst through his reasonable-fatherly façade. 'Let's not worry too much whether the evidence is admissible or valid. Let's not worry whether the man who gives it is a credible witness. Let's just say Lieutenant Petrosino believes it, dispense with the judge, the jury, and the whole goddamn Court, and go out and hang some Eyetalians he suspects of being a secret society!'

He saw the scorn wash off Petrosino, a perfect illustration of the cliché about water and duck's backs. One more time, he sighed, and then the hell with it. 'Let me get it straight now, Joe,' he said wearily. 'Your stool-pigeons tipped you enough to put the pressure on di Primo. You don't say what they told you, by the way, or who they are . . . ' He looked up, the question implicit.

'That's right,' Petrosino said equably.

When he saw that was all he was going to get on the subject, O'Donovan went on: 'You saw di Primo up at Sing Sing. right?'

'With Flynn, the Department of Justice investigator.'

'With Flynn, fine, fine,' agreed O'Donovan. 'Di Primo told you that the murdered man who was found in the barrel in 11th Street was his brother-in-law, Benedetto Madonnia, and that they'd been associated in a counterfeiting operation. Di Primo took a fall, the assumption being that his wife and kids would be looked after by this organization of yours, this Mafia.'

'Specifically, by Lupo, Ignazo Lupo, who was the *capo*.'

'The what?'

'The gang's boss.'

'Oh yeah. I don't understand that Da — that Eyetalian lingo, y'know.'

'I know.'

'Di Primo took a fall to take the heat off the counterfeiting, because the Department of Justice boys were getting too close to it. They figured if someone went down, they'd ease off, give them time to set up someplace else. Here in New York.'

'That's right,' Petrosino said. 'Except for two things. Somewhere higher up, it was decided that the counterfeiting operation was too risky, and Mandonnia was told to close it out. He squawked — he'd be making a lot of money if they went on with it, and so would his brother-in-law, who was presently in Sing Sing to protect them.'

'So this Lupo takes the whole hot potato to arbitration, you say.'

'That's right,' Petrosino confirmed. 'They went to see this Vito Cascio Ferro.

231

He's the top man now in the Mafia.'

'You can prove that?'

'Everybody knows it, Chief.'

'That's not what I asked you.'

'No, I can't prove it,' Petrosino said, exasperation in his voice. 'How would I prove it? You think they give you a badge, like in the Elks?'

'You can't prove it,' O'Donovan said. 'So you can't prove this Ferro and Lupo met, and you can't prove they decided to abolish Madonnia either.'

'Listen, I got the word on the street,' Petrosino said. 'Madonnia threatened to talk, which is fatal in the circles he lived in. Di Primo told us he'd made out some kind of will, or a letter, put it in a safe place in case anything happened to him. The idea was it would give di Primo something to bargain with when he came out of stir.'

'On the street,' O'Donovan said. 'You got this on the street.'

'It's reliable,' Petrosino said. 'My informant's always reliable.'

'You can produce him in court, of course,' O'Donovan sneered.

'Listen, Chief, I've got evidence — all right, not the kind we'd all like, but evidence anyway — that ties Benedetto Madonnia to Vito Ferro and evidence that says Ferro's the man we want above all the rest. He's the top Mafia leader. If we can nail him, we can break the back of this thing before it gets too big. Now why are you giving me such a hard time?'

'*I'm* giving *you* a hard time?' exclaimed O'Donovan. 'You've sure as hell got your nerve, Joe! I've sat here and listened to you going on about your cockamamie evidence, your secret societies and your capo-whatever-they-ares, and tried to point out to you that evidence does not consist of what you picked up from some stool-pigeon on the street, or some con in Sing Sing who'd tell you his grandmother was the Holy Virgin if it'd get his sentence reduced, but you — do you listen? Not a hope! You — you know the rules of evidence as good if not better than any man on the force. Does that stop you? Does it hell! Jumping goddamned Jehosophat, Joe — you haven't got *anything* here! You couldn't even fine those five Eyetalians for spitting on the sidewalk!'

'Hold on, hold on,' Petrosino said. If O'Donovan's outburst had in any way affected him, it didn't show. 'Do you agree there's a demonstrable link between Ferro and Madonnia?'

'If I do, so what?' was the weary reply.

'What about the barrel, then?'

'The barrel?'

'We confirmed that the barrel they found Madonnia's body in was delivered to the Stella d'Italia, a *trattoria* on Elizabeth Street.'

'Sure,' O'Donovan said. 'And you can prove that it was the same one, and not one which had been delivered to this German place on Third Avenue, and even if you can, what does that do to your case against Ferro? Come on, Joe, for Chrissake!'

'Could have, then,' Petrosino said, impatiently. 'It could have been the one. Then there's the sawdust we took from the dead man's trouser cuffs. The lab boys say — '

'The lab boys say it *could* be the same,'

O'Donovan interposed brutally.

'Not is, Joe. Could be.'

'Good God alive, Chief! I know it's circumstantial, but — '

O'Donovan just looked up. When his eyes met Petrosino's the question that the detective had been going to ask died aborning. He knew damned well that O'Donovan wasn't going to play any hunches, back any flyers, take any outside chances, bet on any long odds. O'Donovan wanted cast-iron certainties, or if they weren't available, lead-pipe cinches.

'That does it, Joe,' O'Donovan said. 'This goddamned secret society of yours is just too damned smart for all of us, seems to me. We can't seem to get anything on them at all that'll stand up in court, can we?' The sarcasm in his voice was totally undisguised. 'Some cheap Italian forgers fall out over the split on what they've been printing and you see an international conspiracy. Some two-time loser in the pen spins you his brother-in-law's pipe dreams, and you come up with a dime-novel super-criminal who controls all the other criminals. And for evidence you give me what you hear on the streets!' He leaned back in his chair, breathing heavily, not trying to contain his anger any more. He regarded Petrosino for a long moment from beneath lowered eyebrows. Here it comes, Petrosino thought to himself.

'Joe,' O'Donovan said. 'You better drop this one.'

'Drop it,' Petrosino repeated, no inflexion in his voice.

'Yes, drop it!' O'Donovan snapped, the anger on the edge of his voice sharpening it. 'I had the Mayor on the phone just a couple of hours ago. He's had a delegation from some Italian society, businessmen's league or something. They claimed victimization, Joe. They claimed harrassment. They handed the Mayor a petition signed by more than two thousand people demanding that the persecution of the Italian community by the police in general, and one department of the NYPD in particular, be stopped. They wanted to know — and neither Hizzoner nor I could come up with an answer — how come the Department had an Italian branch but not a Jewish one, or an Irish one, or a German one. They didn't actually name you, Joe, but they came as near as anyone wants them to. This Ferro, whoever he is, the people in the quarter think he's something special.'

'They would,' Petrosino said. 'He's all of that.'

'Well, then,' O'Donovan said, as if Petrosino's words proved his point. 'All the more reason to lay off, Joe. Let things quieten down. It's not as if we haven't got enough on our plates already. Look at this pile here!' He waved a negligent hand at the pile of detective's reports awaiting his perusal. He had to initial each one after reading it. There was a Department legend, no doubt apocryphal, that someone had once sent up a five-page report about an Alsatian dog that had murdered seventeen nuns in the vestry of St Patrick's. O'Donovan had initialled it without comment.

'And if I don't lay off?' Petrosino asked softly.

The Chief of Police looked at him as

though he was some new kind of bug. 'You want me to answer that?' he asked.

Petrosino shook his head. Battering himself bloody against the wall which had so subtly been erected between himself and Vito Ferro was going to achieve nothing. Neither would a head-on collision with the Chief of Police, no matter how stupid Petrosino thought his decisions. That would simply result in suspension, maybe even dismissal. He couldn't fight Ferro out of the Department, and maybe the *mafioso* wasn't the only one who could play politics.

'Good, then,' O'Donovan said, taking the detective's silence for assent. 'We'll call it a day on this Ferro business?'

'Don't have a lot of choice,' Petrosino said, forcing himself to smile in the manner of a brave loser. 'Of course, if I come up with some hard evidence . . . ?

'Why, sure, then we'll take another look at it,' O'Donovan said heartily, rising from his chair and pasting a smile on his face. 'Well, if you'll excuse me, Joe? Lot to do. Work never stops piling up, you know. Yes, never.'

Petrosino had already turned away, so O'Donovan's extended hand was ignored as the detective left the room. Ignorant Dago bastard, the Chief thought as the door closed behind Petrosino's burly back; about time he had his backside kicked good, and by God! he'd had it kicked hard today. He picked up the phone and told Central to put him through to the Mayor's office in City Hall. Jack would be pleased to hear that Petrosino had finally seen sense. With the elections coming up in the Spring, none of them could afford to alienate the massive Italian vote. He let his imagination work on the dramatized version of his talk with Petrosino that he'd tell the Mayor. He felt rather pleased with himself.

★ ★ ★

On November 14, shortly after seven-thirty in the evening, two men went into Salvatore Pignaroza's grubby room on the first floor of the Hester Street tenement. Nobody took any notice of them.

239

Doorbells and janitors had been obsolete in this part of New York for more than twenty years. Tenement hallways were thoroughfares for anyone who cared to use them. Kids played in them all day. Cats yowled in them all night. Drunks slept and urinated and vomited in them. Housewives left their garbage in them. Dogs fought in them. Lovers occasionally fornicated in them. Tenement hallways had a special, persistent, clinging smell, totally their own, immediately identifiable. Once experienced — and experienced was the right verb — the smell was never forgotten by anyone who'd ever been in the peeling, filthy, dank, dark hallways: it was a distillation of all human life. The two men who went quietly up the ravished stairway to Sal Pignaroza's room hardly even noticed the stink. Tenements were nothing new to them.

They knew Pignaroza was in his room because they had been waiting all day for him to return from his penny-ante interests, whatever and wherever they were. Now they came along the filthy

240

uncarpeted hallway and kicked down the half-rotted door of Pignaroza's room. He was lying on the bed with one arm across his eyes, like a man who's done a hard day's work and needs a half-hour rest before getting on with the job of living. He was wearing only vest and pants. He came up off the bed squalling with fright, eyes rolling hugely in fear as he saw the knives in the hands of the two men coming across the room. He looked around him in pure driven desperation but there was nowhere to run, nowhere to hide. The gloomy room didn't even have a window.

Salvatore Pignaroza opened his mouth to scream, but the fear within him was so intense that no sound came from his paralysed vocal chords. Then the two blank-faced killers were on him, their arms rising and falling like automatons. Again, and again, and again, and again, and again, they stabbed the kicking, groaning, figure on the bed, ignoring the leaping gouts of blood which spattered them, ignoring the awful sounds which came from the writhing, mutilated, thing that had been Salvatore Pignaroza, working calmly and methodically and without emotion, like the professional butchers that they were. When they were satisfied that Pignaroza was quite dead, they straightened up, breathing heavily, the sound they made harsh in the darkened room. Then one of them bent down and ripped away the bloodstained pants, standing back while the other went to work again with the knife.

★　★　★

Almost twenty-four hours passed before Pignaroza's body was discovered. During that time, certain inmates at Sing Sing prison learned to their surprise that they had visitors whom they had not been expecting. These unexpected visitors were quietly spoken, self-effacing 'cousins' newly arrived from the Old Country, who had out of familial love and duty made the long journey up the Hudson to Ossining to see their dear ones. Ah, the embraces, the *abbracios*, the fond hugs and kisses! These were all strictly forbidden, of course, but the guards turned a blind eye. After all, these people had come all the way from Italy, and the least they could do was to allow them a proper greeting. Especially since the visitors had so very generously greased their palms, nodding and winking in the friendliest fashion. It would have been almost inhuman not to let them have their happy moment together, wouldn't it? Besides, they were so well-behaved, such obviously decent people.

And when visiting hours were over, and the visitors departed, the prisoners returned to their cells with weapons which had been passed to them concealed in the legs or arms of their baggy striped uniforms. Small though the knives were, they were razor-sharp and wickedly pointed, easy to hide in any one of half a dozen places. Needless to say, the convicts had no difficulty in doing just that. Or in concealing them about themselves when they came out into the exercise yard the next day.

It was a cold, grey, unfriendly day, with a pushy wind bustling up the Hudson from the Atlantic, bringing the grey smell of snow with it. The convicts swung their arms, flailing them across their chests to keep as warm as they could, trotting around the yard, their feet clattering on the cobbles, wary-eyed guards watching them indolently from the watchtowers around the walls. Balloons of condensation hung in the still air. The sound of heavy breathing made by men unused to more than nominal exercise, muted amid the rattle of hobnailed boots on the stone yard; the shouts of the guards as sharp as drill-sergeants — all echoed off the mighty concrete walls and up towards the unheeding flat grey sky.

When the whistle blew for assembly, all the convicts bunched together as they jostled into line before being returned to the comparative warmth of their cells. There was always the same seeming confusion, always the same few moments when the exercise yard, seen from above, looked like nothing so much as a fisherman's bait-tin, packed with a seething, grey-striped mob slowly assuming disciplined lines as the convicts dressed right like recruits in an army camp.

Except that today when the lines formed, the guards saw that a man lay slumped in a huddled heap at one side of the faceless yard near the frowning concrete walls. A guard blew his whistle and three others came immediately, running at the double towards the trouble-spot, batons drawn, hands on pistols, ready for anything. They clustered around the kneeling guard and saw the spreading pool of bright blood, the ragged stab wounds on face and neck and chest and belly of the huddled corpse. Looking up, around, they saw only the sightless, expressionless eyes of the waiting convicts: men patently certain to have seen, and heard, absolutely nothing untoward whatsoever.

'Dead?' one of the guards asked. He didn't really need to ask. The man on the floor of the exercise yard lay peculiarly close to the ground, the way no breathing creature can.

'As Moses,' said the kneeling guard, putting a hand on his knee and levering

245

himself upright. 'And there'll be all hell to pay now!' He walked to the line of prisoners nearby and glared at them, as though his menacing stare could make them speak. 'All right!' he snapped. 'Now what the hell happened here?'

Their faces told him nothing. Their eyes remained fixed front, unseeing. Nobody made a sound, nobody so much as even twitched an eyelid. The guard turned away from them in disgust and looked down at the figure of the dead man.

'Hell to pay,' he repeated.

'Who is it, Kitch?' one of his colleagues asked.

'Di Primo,' Kitch said sourly. 'Giuseppe di Primo.'

'Oh, Christ!' said the other guard.

★ ★ ★

The foreman at the slate quarry told Caterina Abruzzo, as kindly as he knew how, that her husband probably never felt a thing. He'd been working at the foot of the quarry among a squad of men

246

shovelling the broken slate away from the face. It was day-labourer's work and not over-well paid, but Giovanni Abruzzo had been down on his luck. Why, he'd not really known. It was just that doors which had been open to him for as long as he could recall were suddenly closed. So the job at the quarry out on Staten Island was better than no job at all and he'd at least made enough to eat, enough to tide them over until times got better. But times never got better. There was a shale slide, a sudden, enormous movement of perhaps two hundred tons of rubble and rock that unaccountably toppled over the edge of the quarry and rained down upon the spot where Giovanni Abruzzo stood. He had no business being there at all, in fact, the foreman told Caterina. He was supposed to be with the rest of the men further along the face. Be all that as it may, he was just as dead; and when, two days later, they managed to dig out his body, they prevailed upon his widow to let them put it into a sealed coffin and take it straight to the cemetery. She never knew that what she had buried was in fact a sandbag into which they had put as much of Giovanni Abruzzo as they had managed to scrape off the rock. Nor did it ever occur to her that what had happened was anything other than a terrible accident.

★ ★ ★

Lieutenant Joe Petrosino knew, of course.

He knew who'd killed Salvatore Pignaroza; who'd arranged for the inexplicable death of Giuseppe di Primo; who'd set up Giovanni Abruzzo's death to look like an accident. He knew, all right. But there wasn't a solitary damned thing he could do about it.

11

You had to hand it to Petrosino, Flynn thought.

Call it whatever you like that had flattened him: Luck, Fate, Providence, the mills of God — whatever it was, he'd never seen a man knocked down harder. Yet Petrosino had got up off the floor, dusted off his clothes, pasted a determined look on his face, and waded in all over again.

You couldn't like Petrosino, Flynn had decided. First, he wouldn't let anyone that close. He was much too much inside himself, dreaming whatever dreams a man like Petrosino dreamed. Second, you'd have to want to like him and by God! it was hard to. He recalled the times he'd damned near bitten through the stem of his pipe in sheer frustration at Petrosino's unstudied rudeness, and worse, his complete lack of tact with everyone else. There were some people you just had to play differently to others if you wanted to stay alive in everyday society. Petrosino played them all the same way: badly.

He realized that whatever insight his association with the detective had given him into Petrosino's character, it made the man no more endearing than he'd been before, which wasn't very; but for all that, you had to at least respect a man who believed so completely in his own ultimate rightness and worked so hard to make everyone else finally acknowledge it. And do it without admitting the need for help of any kind. He knew, and Flynn knew he knew, that Flynn had superior knowledge by simple virtue of what he did, where he did it, and the length of time he'd been doing it. Petrosino just plain wouldn't recognize it; he'd ignore it, wait until Flynn had to volunteer the information without which he couldn't proceed, and then proceed as if he'd always had that information, never once acknowledging that it had been given to him. Ho hum, Flynn thought, I've been through all this too many damned times to go through it again. The big problem now is Petrosino himself.

Flynn regarded the problem as objectively as he could. As the *in situ* representative of the Attorney-General of the United States, he believed — and therefore the Attorney-General believed — that, whatever you called it: Black Hand or Camorra or Mafia or some combination of all three, there was a nationwide organization, a cartel of crime, loosely linked by nationality — Italian — and that it was considerably too large and too powerful to be taken on single-handed by a lieutenant of the New York Police Department, however dedicated, however single-minded. The Department of Justice was a lot more interested in charting the waters in which the school of fish swam than in hooking any particular fish, no matter how big a fish it was. Petrosino only wanted one man: the man who had bested him.

It might, Flynn reflected, have been bearable if they'd come in the night to kill Petrosino, but they hadn't done that. They hadn't worked him over in some alley so he'd have the badges of his own courage to wear. They hadn't threatened Petrosino's life, thrown bombs at him, sent him anonymous letters; nothing like that. What they had done was to make him look small and ineffectual. The wound was a much more savage and much deeper one than any scar on flesh: it was subtle, cunning, sly. It removed the source of Petrosino's strength and pride: his connexions in the quarter. It rendered him impotent. Petrosino could prowl the streets of Little Italy until he was purple and no one down there would so much as give him the time. The word was out: talk with the Dago and you get what Pignaroza got, what Abruzzi got, what di Primo got. They'd done their job well.

Flynn himself no longer doubted who 'they' were. His eyes ranged almost casually along the rows of box files on the shelf to his right. There were eighteen of them, all innocuously labelled COR-RESPONDENCE / MISCELLANEOUS.

Some of them, about six, were truly nothing more than that. All the others were reports, notes, rundowns, descriptions, ID sheets — the fruits of four years' work by himself and other Department of Justice Investigators in major cities throughout America. They contained treatises by learned historians on the origins and customs of the Honoured Society. They contained documents and descriptions by half a hundred men who had seen the results of the Mafia at work: from New York in the late seventies and early eighties; from New Orleans in the 1890s when the Matranga brothers who'd run the waterfront had assassinated the Chief of New Orleans Police and sparked off a wave of race riots throughout the country. From Pittsburgh in Pennsylvania to Chicago, from the San Francisco waterfront to the stews of St Louis, Missouri, had come the traces of the *alianza*. In the affidavits of longshoremen and market workers, truck farmers and storekeepers, whores and bricklayers, fishermen and assassins who'd testified to the hold which the *mafiosi* had on the underbelly of America. File after file after file, he thought wryly, beautifully cross-indexed and thumb-referenced, the whole boiling — except for one thing: not one single, solitary goddamned word from anyone who'd admit to ever having been a member of the Mafia, being married to one, the brother, sister, uncle, aunt, cousin, father or mother of one, the wife of one, the sweetheart of one, not even the drinking companion of one. And until we get such an affidavit, he thought, it's going to be mighty tough to get anyone to believe that such an organization truly exists.

He thought back over the cases he'd handled in his years with the Justice Department. He'd come in not long after being admitted to the Bar, qualified as a lawyer but without any other experience at all. They soon gave you training, though: the Department had a tradition of training its people that went back to the days when they'd had investigators out on the frontier who carried their own law with them, a statute book in one saddlebag and a sixgun in the other. Such men — the infamous Gus Wells, or Frank Angel — had become legend, as the Department of Justice grew from a hand-me-down branch of the legislative arm stuck in a rackety old building on Pennsylvania Avenue to the overall judicial and investigative branch of the Government. Nowadays there were over fifty special investigators, as well as legal experts, land experts, transportation experts, financial experts, men with every conceivable kind of special knowledge, there to be called on by any member of the Department. And none of it the slightest use in trying to breach the wall of silence which surrounded the Mafia, he thought.

He went across to the window of his office. The new Custom House in which it was situated had been opened only a short while and people were still coming down Broadway to State Street where they could stand and gawp up at the Daniel Chester French sculptures depicting the four continents, and the statues above them representing the world's most famous trading cities. His own favourite was the Doge with the death's head, who represented Venice. In his own mind, he'd already equated the macabre figure with Palermo. Out across Castle Garden he could see sailboats plying across the harbour, and the slim shape of the Statue of Liberty in the haze across the bay. 'Give me your huddled masses yearning to be free,' he said softly. There were millions and millions of Italians living in America. Only a tiny fraction of one per cent of them were criminals. Some of them are citizens so upright they'd hum like a tuning-fork if you tapped them.

He found himself thinking about Joe Petrosino again.

Why the hell do I feel sorry for him? he wondered. He's obnoxious, he's disliked, he's patronizing, he's dull, he hasn't any sense of humour you could detect, and latterly he's been as touchy as a pregnant rattlesnake. Why feel he needs sympathy?

Maybe because of how what had happened had hit the detective, he thought. He'd been in Petrosino's office when the word came in that they'd found Pignaroza's body. The patrolman who found him didn't know it was Salvatore Pignaroza, not at first. He couldn't understand more than one word in twenty of the stream of Italian the landlord was spewing at him. All he knew was that he had a stiff who'd been seen off in exactly the same way as the 'man in the barrel' who'd made all the headlines not long ago. So he called in from the street phone and the detectives got down to Hester Street. They took a good look at the diabolical mess in the sleazy room and said what they always said at times like this: 'Get Petrosino down here!'

The call to Petrosino was placed, and he, Flynn, had watched the detective put down the telephone with a strange, stunned look on his face.

'Joe?' Flynn said after long moments of silence. 'What is it?'

'Uh?'

'What is it?'

Petrosino got up from behind his desk

as in a dream, then shook his head angrily. Then, as if some other, stronger part of him had reasserted its dominance, he became all action, all haste. 'Sounds as if they've killed Sal Pignaroza,' he said. 'The address fits, anyway.'

He was already on his way to the door, and by the time they got downstairs there was a paddy-wagon waiting. They piled in and the driver whacked the horses into a hell-for-leather run, the bell clanging frantically to clear the crowded street, Flynn and Petrosino hanging on to the straps inside as if on some demented streetcar. There was a crowd outside the tenement when they arrived, and they clustered around to see the new arrivals, jostling the steaming horses.

'Get the hell back, there!' shouted the patrolmen, as they saw Petrosino. There were some jeers, one or two half-hearted boos, but by and large it was a sporting crowd which was treating the murder of Salvatore Pignaroza as a mildly interesting diversion in a generally humdrum sort of week. Petrosino pushed roughly through the gawkers, Flynn on his heels, badge pinned to his lapel. They ran up the stoop and upstairs.

The room was like a charnel-house and Flynn recoiled from the sight of the thing on the bed. You got used to seeing dead men: it was a by-product of the job. But the savagery here was almost demoniacal and he took long minutes to realize that the dead man was indeed the same Salvatore Pignaroza whom he'd last seen drinking beer in the Bowery saloon. The face was bloated with the bloody flesh that had been stuffed into it, the eyes still staring, the terror fixed on the face as if in a photograph. There were sticky blobs of half-dry blood everywhere, on the furniture and the floor and the ceiling and the wall behind the bed: Pignaroza's body looked almost shrivelled as though every one of his seven pints of blood had been spilled in this stinking room. The ME was standing in the hallway talking to the patrolman who'd found the body. Petrosino came out and nodded.

'Doc,' he said.

'Oh, hello, Petrosino,' the ME said. He didn't sound as if he was glad to see the detective. Nobody had, Flynn thought.

'Flynn, Department of Justice,' he said, extending a hand. He'd worked with Petrosino enough to know that there'd be no introduction unless he forced it. Petrosino wanted to meet all your contacts, but he very, very, rarely let you get chummy with any of his.

'Department of Justice, eh?' the ME said. 'You interested in this?' He jerked his head at the body inside the room.

'Just along for the ride, Doctor . . . ?'

'Cook,' the ME said, 'Fred Cook.'

'Glad to know you.'

'Sure. He a friend of yours, Petrosino?' Cook asked.

'Name's Pignaroza,' Petrosino said. He said it like a man who doesn't want to believe an unpalatable fact. Well, he sure as hell was going to have to believe this one, Flynn thought. They didn't come any deader than Salvatore Pignaroza. He watched as Petrosino spelled out the name for Cook to enter in his casebook.

'You knew him, then?' Cook asked.

'Sort of,' Petrosino said. 'What have we got?'

'Damn all, as far as I can tell,' Cook said. 'Killed some time between late afternoon and midnight last night's as close as I can come without an autopsy. You can see what the cause of death was,' he added drily.

'That how you found the body, Frank?' Petrosino asked the patrolman.

'Sure thing, Lieutenant,' the patrolman said. 'Right there on the bed.'

'Nothing on him?' Petrosino persisted. 'No note pinned to his clothes, anything like that?'

'Nope,' the patrolman said, shaking his head.

'What he did have in his pockets is on the table there,' Cook put in, pointing with his chin. There was a folding card-table standing near the wall. On it were what paltry possessions Salvatore Pignaroza had bequeathed to an uncaring world: seventy or eighty cents in change; two grubby ten dollar bills and three singles; a key ring with one key on it; a pocket comb; a handkerchief; a folded oilskin pouch of the kind seamen carried, which contained Pignaroza's cigarette papers and tobacco. And that was it.

'You taking charge of this, Petrosino?' Cook asked.

The Italian nodded, his dark face completely expressionless.

'Okay if I get the stiff over to the Morgue? We can fill in the DOA form and get on with the autopsy. I'll send it over to you.'

'Sure,' Petrosino said, his mind elsewhere. 'Thanks, Doc.'

Flynn watched the detective, puzzled by his reaction. Pignaroza's death was obviously intended, as had been that of Madonnia, both to shut him up and serve as a warning to those with loose tongues. Petrosino, however, was acting as if the end of the world had just been announced.

'Come on, Joe,' he found himself saying. 'I'll buy you a drink.'

'Uh?' Petrosino said. 'Oh. All right.'

He took a last look around the room as though wanting to commit it to memory, and then they went out into the hallway.

The patrolman gave a perfunctory salute. As they came down the stoop, a man in a tight-fitting dark suit carrying a notebook pushed towards Petrosino.

'Hey, Joe!' he shouted. 'Petrosino! Remember me, Atkins from the *Tribune*?'

Petrosino's head came up: he looked just like a fighting bull who's seen something he can charge, Flynn thought.

'What's the story in there, Joe?' Atkins said, getting close to Petrosino's right elbow. 'You got a statement for me?'

He was only a small man, not at all powerfully built, and he literally turned white as Petrosino roared, bellowed, letting all the anger in him come out in his voice. 'Get the hell away from me!' shouted Petrosino. He half raised his arm as though to strike the reporter, and the man fell back, cowering in fear, scuttling out of range and back into the crowd, his face wearing the astonished expression of someone who's just been attacked by a teddy bear.

Flynn took hold of Petrosino's arm. The detective was trembling with suppressed anger, and Flynn hustled him away from the gaping throng of onlookers, ignoring the puzzled look of the patrolman. He walked Petrosino up Hester Street, pushing through crowds jostling for bargains from pushcart peddlers trying to clear their stocks before nightfall, and when they got to Broadway, turned uptown. They went up Broadway, past Lord & Taylor's wholesale place and the St Nicholas Hotel. There was a saloon two doors past there and Flynn steered Petrosino inside, signalling to the bartender for two whiskies. He watched in silence as the man slapped two shot glasses on the bar with practised ease and plonked a bottle in front of them. Flynn poured. Petrosino stared at the drink as if it was likely to turn into a rhinoceros.

'Joe,' Flynn said, 'what the hell is it?'

Petrosino looked at him and Flynn felt a small shock of astonishment: there were signs in the dark eyes that in anyone else he would have sworn were the beginning of tears.

'You don't understand, Bill,' Petrosino said.

'Sure I understand,' Flynn said.

'Pignaroza was killed off because he was an informer. You said yourself that was how they treated informers. It means you've got them worried.'

'No it doesn't,' Petrosino said dully.

'Well, what, for God's sake?'

'Listen to me,' Petrosino said. 'They killed him on my territory, Bill. Right in the middle of the quarter. That's the same as if they'd cut him up and sent him to me in a parcel.'

'Yes,' Flynn said, encouragingly.

'Christ, Flynn,' Petrosino said, exasperation coming into his voice. 'They killed Sal on my patch, stuffed his prick in his mouth to shut him up! In Little Italy that's the same as if they'd put up a hoarding with letters six feet high saying 'Anyone talking to Petrosino gets the same.' '

'Ah,' Flynn said.

'You're damned right, ah,' Petrosino said, slopping more whisky into his glass and tipping it down his throat as if it were cough medicine.

'But Madonnia got it the same way,' Flynn objected. 'Nobody suggested his killing was aimed at you.'

'That's because it wasn't,' Petrosino said. 'You want another of these?' When Flynn shook his head, Petrosino poured himself another drink. 'Wasn't aimed at me,' he went on. 'Madonnia wasn't one of my people. Pignaroza was. One of *my* people, and by now you can bet everyone in the quarter knows he was. Which means that we got too close. Someone put the blocks on. They'll all clam up down there, now. I ask someone the way on Mulberry Street, they'll misdirect me.'

Flynn let out a short laugh. Even Petrosino couldn't believe this!

'Christ, Joe,' he said. 'You've got other sources than poor old Sal Pignaroza!'

'You'll see,' Petrosino said darkly. 'You'll see. Another?'

'For the road,' Flynn suggested, as Petrosino poured again. It sure as hell isn't my job to cheer him up, he thought. You can bet every cent you've got in the Washington Savings & Loan Association that if the day ever comes when Bill Flynn needs cheering up the last one in line will be Lieutenant Petrosino.

'For the road,' Petrosino said. 'If you got to.'

Flynn managed to grin. Somehow it was coming out as him spoiling Petrosino's evening, despite the fact that the detective had swigged down five drinks to his two. Hell with it! he thought.

They got back to Police Headquarters with just a mild buzz on, at least closer to *cameraderie* than not. Petrosino had his normal colour back, and by now Flynn was sure he must have imagined the threat of tears, for there was nothing but business in the dark Italian eyes.

As they went into the Mulberry Street building, the desk sergeant called Flynn's name. 'Message for you, Bill,' he said. He handed Flynn a slip of paper, and Flynn read the message on it with, at first, astonishment, then an awful feeling of inevitability, of something almost pre-ordained.

He passed it without a word to Petrosino, who looked at Flynn's face for a clue, then read the message aloud. 'Giuseppe di Primo fatally stabbed,' he muttered. 'Please contact the Warden at Sing Sing immediately.' Petrosino crumpled the paper into a ball in his hand. His mouth was like a slit in a steel plate. 'Well, great, Flynn,' he rasped. 'Just goddamned great!' He turned and stalked away, leaving Flynn gaping at his retreating back.

There'd been plenty of times when he'd misinterpreted Petrosino's words, discovering later that the Italian had meant something totally different. But not this time. Petrosino's tone, his inference, had been unmistakable: there was no damned point in his asking anyone to do anything. They'd always screw it up. Only he, Petrosino, was infallible. Flynn had had his chance, and see what happened?

Flynn shook his head. He saw the desk sergeant looking at him with a sympathetic grin waiting to be born. He shrugged, and the sergeant let the grin blossom. 'We been placin' bets,' he said.

'How's that?' Flynn asked.

'The boys in the squadroom,' the desk sergeant explained. 'We been layin' bets how long it would be before you got shafted.'

'Oh,' said Flynn, seeing them doing it in his mind's eye. 'How'd I make out?'

'If it's any consolation,' the desk sergeant told him, 'you beat the world record.'

'But it was only a matter of time, right?'

'Right. He shafts everyone in the end.'

'Ever wondered why?' Flynn asked, defending Petrosino without knowing why he was doing it.

'Not me, brother,' said the sergeant. 'I'm just sitting here waiting for the day someone does it to him.'

⋆   ⋆   ⋆

Over the next few months Petrosino threw himself into his work with an almost religious fervour. There was no lead too slender for him to follow up personally, no piece of information upon which he did not batten with the frenzy of desperation. But he was getting nowhere and he knew it. Hearing about him, Flynn knew it. And slowly the word filtered upstairs so that the Chief of Police and the Commissioners and the Mayor knew it, too. Petrosino was becoming something of an albatross around their necks, and with the streets of Little Italy closed as firmly in his face as are the gates of Paradise to Satan, he was like a man with a worn-out broom trying to shift ten miles of sandhills.

Give him his due, he never admitted defeat.

When he wasn't chasing around, Petrosino was writing long and detailed outlines and propositions to Commissioner Bingham, to his old acquaintance Teddy Roosevelt, now President of the United States, and to Congressmen and Senators and newspapermen with whom he could claim some kind of friendship. He was convinced — having heard every facet of each of his arguments many, many times, Flynn knew why he was convinced — that the way to get inside the Mafia was to go to Italy and check with the law-enforcement agencies there on every known criminal who had emigrated from Italy to the United States. There would be dossiers, he told them all. Armed with these, the American government could implement plans to deport as undesirable aliens all those who had come to America with undeclared criminal records.

He had it all worked out: boat and train fares, hotel costs, incidental expenses, a complete itinerary with the names of every official he planned to try and see: Lloyd Grissom, American Ambassador in Rome, Camillo Peano, Minister of the Interior, Francesco Leonardi, Chief of Police in Rome, and so on — in Naples and finally in Palermo. He got through reams and reams and reams of correspondence, a man possessed, exorcizing demons only he knew existed.

The more he embroiled himself in his new crusade, the less Flynn got to see of Petrosino. Their relationship had cooled dramatically on the night that they had learned of di Primo's assassination, but Flynn had been partially forgiven after the discovery that Giovanni Abruzzo had also been silenced, and in a manner for which not even Petrosino could blame the Department of Justice agent. Even so, they saw little of each other. Whenever Flynn went uptown, Petrosino was either out, or so immersed in scribbling on the yellow ruled legal foolscap paper he invariably used for his letters that he would be impossible to talk with, and sometimes waved Flynn away with an impatient gesture such as a parent might use to dismiss an importunate child.

Flynn would stand outside the door of Petrosino's office, the doorknob still in his hand, and count to twenty so that he would not finally explode and barge back in, grab Petrosino's shirtfront in his fist, haul the Italian out of his chair, and beat seven different kinds of cowshit out of him. Then he'd shrug. If he marched in right now and did just that, Petrosino would never really understand why. So he'd let the anger dissipate in a wry wisecrack, or just leave, go get a cup of coffee somewhere and contemplate more eternal verities.

Joe Petrosino never came down to the Custom House to see him. And after a while Flynn quit calling in on the offchance at Mulberry Street. He had plenty of other work to occupy him, and the Italian thing was very quiet, very low-profiled right now. This work involved less and less the need to tramp up the flights of stairs to Petrosino's smoke-filled office, less and less to help the detective shape his curiously stilted and sometimes hilariously misguided phraseology into more readable English for his reports and letters. Anyway, he told himself, Petrosino didn't need him. Maybe he'd be better off working his own way out of the mess he was in. Flynn did it with Petrosino's best interests at heart; and by trying to help Petrosino less, he brought about his downfall by helping too much.

The Department of Justice had a long arm. That its investigations would finally rebound so catastrophically upon Joe Petrosino, Flynn had no way of knowing, of course. Had he had such an inkling, he might have followed through the lead himself. As it was, when it turned up, he passed it to Petrosino.

Purely as a matter of course, Flynn was sent copies of all Departmental reports dealing with what was called internally 'the Italian investigation.' So it came about one day that he received a copy of a report by Daniel Askew, Special Investigator of the Department of Justice, who had interviewed a Mrs Graziella Madonnia in connexion with the inquiries he was still making into the whereabouts and identities of the gang of counterfeiters of whom one had been the late unlamented Giuseppe di Primo. It was the name Madonnia which caught Flynn's eye, and he read it more carefully than he might otherwise have done. Mrs Graziella Madonnia was the wife of the murdered Benedetto Madonnia, and as he read the report, somewhere buried deep in the memory cells of his brain Flynn sensed a signal blinking. Something he had seen somewhere, a connexion, a link, a small fact. But what? He read the relevant paragraph from Askew's report again.

at that time. Mrs Madonnia said she could not see how her husband could have been involved in printing or distributing counterfeit money since he never seemed to have any money and never sent her any. If anything, it was the other way around. Said that Madonnia had even pawned the watch which her father had given him on their wedding day and she didn't expect to see it again, since she didn't have the money to redeem the pawn with the ticket that had been sent back to her with his effects.

Mrs Madonnia went on to state that her husband had known he was in danger. Friends in New York and elsewhere had got word to him through her and through her brother, Giuseppe di Primo. She would not say who these friends were. Would not say exactly what the information she passed to her husband was. Would not say from whom or what source the danger to her husband came.

Subsequent to this interview, Mrs Madonnia was forced to quit the house she had been renting and move to an apartment at 22 – 20 Laurel Street. She expressed willingness to be questioned further should the necessity arise, but

Flynn put the report down on his desk and stared at it. Nothing in it that he had not known already. Or was there? What, then, what, what? Instantly, the subtle tendrils of memory told him that he knew something, that he had a connexion. But what? He went to the row of box files and pulled one out, opening it and leafing through the pages until he found his own report on the murder of Benedetto Madonnia. It had been mostly based on Petrosino's, and told him nothing. No click. Across the bottom of the report he had scrawled in his sprawling handwriting: *October 31 1906. Petrosino arrested Giuseppe Morello, Giuseppe Fontana, Vito Ferro, Tommaso Petto, Antonio Lombrado, for m of Madonnia. All released on bail. GM $5000, GF $5000, VF $1000 TP $3000, AL $2000. QV.*

Qui vide, he thought, still nagged by that something at the back of his memory. Something. What? What had triggered the response? He read Askew's report again. What was it? Watch, his mind said. The watch! Pawned the watch! Pawnshop! Pawn ticket!

He riffled impatiently through the arrest records that he had filed after the *débâcle* in which Paul le Barbier had wafted his clients out of the Tombs. In the course of their arrest, all five prisoners had been stripped and searched, the contents of their pockets turned over to the desk sergeant while they were in the cells. They would have been returned in the familiar brown envelope upon their release.

He checked Morello's file.

Nothing.

Fontana, the same. Ferro, likewise. One by one, carefully, methodically, he checked and re-checked until finally, on the arrest record of Tommaso 'the Bull' Petto, he found what he was looking for. It was a possibility, far-fetched enough, but a possibility; so fragile that he was scared to test its strength. In the list of Tommaso Petto's belongings, all returned to him when he was released on 1 November 1906, was the following entry:

PLEDGE TICKET NUMBER 2335.
FROM ABRAHAMS & SONS, 233

BOWERY, AGAINST ONE GENTLE-
MAN'S GOLD-PLATED HUNTER
WATCH.

It couldn't be, he told himself. It couldn't
be. They must have checked it. Then: why
would they check it? It would be just a
pawn ticket. It's a coincidence, that's all.
There must be thousands of pawn tickets
for thousands of gold-plated watches.
Madonnia's watch? If only the desk
sergeant had written down the date of the
pledge! Boy, he thought to himself, you
really want it on a plate. Yet still he
hesitated to pick up the telephone. If he
was wrong, Petrosino would give him the
horse-laugh and he'd had about enough
of getting the horse-laugh from that
particular nag. Yet . . . suppose it was a
real lead, a concrete connexion between
Petto and Madonnia? Murder was not his
brief — that was the job of the local
police, and Petrosino in particular, since
it was his case. The establishing of a
connexion between a dead *mafioso* and a
live one, however, very much *was* Flynn's
responsibility. What to do? Follow it up

himself, or give the battered Petrosino a chance? Christ! he thought, I'm acting like a kid. He picked up the phone.

★   ★   ★

Most cops weren't on the take.

Well, put it his way — not *exactly* what you'd call on the take. Most cops justified their own perks by defining grafts as coming in two kinds: there was clean graft and 'dirty' graft. Very few of them got involved with the second kind. It had a nasty habit of marking your hands, so that when some crusader — and there were getting to be more and more of them each year — alleged police corruption, and the boys upstairs needed someone's head to hand to him on a plate, then the cop who'd been taking 'dirty' graft was it. It was too easy to spot, 'dirty' graft; too easy to nail down the cop who looked the other way when he was told to, was elsewhere when necessary, took longer than necessary to report some felony. Everyone on the force knew there were cops like that. They were the ones the

Commissioners referred to when, during or after some new allegation of corruption in the Department, they told the public and the Press that it was just one or two bad apples which were rotting the good ones in the barrel.

Most cops weren't on the take, then, in that way. But the clean graft — nobody really thought very much about it at all. A cop who looked after his beat, kept the streets clean, or a captain who ran a tight precinct, everything shipshape: these didn't think it amiss to accept presents of cash or kind from grateful local merchants, storekeepers who didn't have to spend half of their working day watching out for shoplifters, apartment-house dwellers who could sleep relatively securely in their beds and not fear footpads or burglars, bookies happy to make their drop into the station-house bag. That wasn't real graft, man, that was a sort of lubrication, necessary to keep the wheels turning smoothly. It was clean graft.

Some cops, of course, wouldn't even take clean graft.

Some cops would beat in the head of any man who offered them a bribe or any kind of gratuity on the simple principle that nobody ever gives anybody anything for nothing. Some cops kept their beats clean because that was what the city paid them to do, and they'd run anyone who said differently in so fast that their asses would scorch the sidewalk. A good cop signed up to enforce the law, and there were some cops who did just that.

Some cops, maybe. But not Georgie Dicks. Georgie Dicks was a third-generation cop, the only one on the New York force, and that made him something kind of special. His grandfather, Lawrence Dicks, had risen to the rank of sergeant in the early days when Tom Byrnes had been a patrolman — and a damned nuisance because he not only wouldn't take a bribe but he kept blowing the whistle on everyone else who did. Georgie's father, George Robert Dicks, had been inspector of the First District right up to the time of his death, and both men had been honest cops in the sense that neither had at any time ever touched 'dirty' graft. Inspector Dicks, throughout his long career, had always insisted that his patrolmen never hustle anyone, always remaining within the unwritten boundaries of the unspoken agreement. He educated his son to appreciate that, as long as nobody pushed too hard, there was plenty for everyone. Enough for Georgie to go to college, enough for the family to live comfortably in a big old frame-house with its own backyard out in Brooklyn. Nothing fancy, you understand: just a serene middle class life of quiet gentility such as their lace-curtain Irish forebears would have gasped to see. There were never any ghettos in the life of Georgie Dicks, no tenements. He joined the Department straight from college, a new kind of cop, an educated one. His rise was steady, perhaps slightly faster than others who were his equals felt was justifiable, but then, Georgie Dicks was something of a showpiece, a grandson and son of highly respected New York cops.

Georgie, however, was on the take. 'In the bag', as they said at Tammany. There were a lot of cops in the bag at any given moment, of course. All ranks, from inspectors right on down to the lowest rookie on the beat. At some time or other, every cop was approached. It was all a question of temperament, percentages. Often the approach drew a roar of rage and perhaps even a broken head for some go-between. Sometimes — often enough — it didn't.

Georgie Dicks had never really thought of the take from the Precinct bag as the sum of his ambitions. Thank-you presents from some shopkeeper who'd been allowed to overlook a street regulation or a zoning ordnance, five bucks here and ten bucks there, that wasn't Georgie's idea of getting rich. Georgie knew what rich was, and he wanted some. In fact he wanted all of it: the big house up near the Park, the lovely gewgaws you could buy on Fifth Avenue, the trotting horses, the country place, the servants, the champagne, the cigars. He wasn't going to be a punk police captain all his goddamned life, and he let that be known here and there, bringing gratified smiles to certain faces in certain places.

Georgie had been on the take for some years down in his own precinct, the Fifth, and as the swelling tide of immigration had turned Little Italy into a seething goldmine of possibilities, Georgie had waxed gradually richer. Here and there, he allowed it to be known that the Captain was a reasonable man, approachable, a man who would always listen to, shall we say, persuasion. The years went by, and Captain Georgie Dicks got richer.

He ran his precinct well. His superiors were happy with his results, for the Fifth had one of the rougher parts of town to handle. It was good public relations to have Dicks in charge of it, and to be able to say to the newpapers that the family standards were as high as they had ever been. Georgie Dicks worked to become indispensable, knowing that if he kept his nose half-way clean he'd retire as an inspector, with a comfortable pile. His superiors let him become indispensable, not knowing about his pile, but knowing that Georgie's inspectorship was, all things remaining equal, as inevitable as next January. Meanwhile, they left him to run his precinct and were glad he did it so well. He was a big, tough, mean man, Georgie Dicks. Just what they needed down there.

His favours weren't cheap, not a bit of it. Once Georgie got the hang of things, you had to pay for his favours. But there was a man of the people at Tammany who was prepared to pay for certain freedoms in the streets of Little Italy, certain guarantees that some other men of the people might find it hard to canvass there come election time, for instance. There was a man who owned a chain of brothels, really Fancy-Dan places with a good clientele, which were a natural mark for the street gangs either to heist or put the black on. He was happy, this brothelkeeper, to put up the money for Georgie's reassurance that any punk who tried to put the arm on Dutchy Heimberger would get his head broken. One or two heads were duly broken to make the point, and the rest got the message. Heimberger's business boomed, and Georgie benefited accordingly. He was drawing a pension now, monthly, which made his captain's salary look like the money for the dog's meat.

He lived in a nice little house over on West 9th Street, near Sixth. He collected foreign stamps because someone had told him they were a good hedge against inflation, and then he'd gotten hooked. He had all the paraphernalia, magnifying glasses and tweezers, glassine envelopes and sticky paper hinges, and three big loose-leaf albums that didn't shut properly because there were so many stamps in them. He liked German stamps the best, and after them French ones. They gave him a sense of the martial grandeur of Europe that he admired. One day he was going to do the Grand Tour.

The one thing that nobody knew about Georgie Dicks was that he also worked for Don Gabriele Pantucci. Nobody knew anything about it, or how the relationship had come about, and nobody ever would, not even Georgie Dicks's wife, because Georgie Dicks was too ashamed to even mention it. The old man in the little house on Charlton Street had known, of course. That flat-eyed bastard Lombrado, who Dicks hated so much, had also known. And, of course, Don Vito had known later. Not that he, or Lombrado, would ever speak of it. Yet the fact that they *knew* was a cancer in Georgie Dicks's bones, and if he had possessed the guts of a butterfly he would have thrown off their shackles. They were nothing but dago thugs, he knew that. He was still terrified of them.

He could not say it aloud, could not admit it to any other living human being, but he was terrified of them. They were not like the carefree, sunny-dispositioned Italians you passed the time of day with on the stoops of the tenements in the quarter, the ones who loved to feel the warm sun on their faces, the soft tang of wine on their tongues. These Sicilians were different altogether, as cruel and indifferent as the land of their birth.

He had been approached first by Don Gabriele's *consigliere*, Lombrado. Quietly dressed, softly spoken, Lombrado had come deferentially to Dicks's house and asked to speak with him. When he'd realized what the guinea bastard was actually leading up to, Dicks had gone wild. He had knocked Lombrado down, then lifted him to his feet and knocked him down again, and kept on doing it while Lombrado offered not even a token resistance. Dicks had cursed and sworn and punished the man's face with his ham-like hands for coming to his house and suggesting that he, the son and the grandson of men of honour and dignity, would accept bribes! And at that from some goddamned Dago Knife-thrower! His rage had been genuine: he basically disliked foreigners, and Italians in particular. He felt in his heart, and sometimes said to his wife, that they were like a swarm of rats overrunning the city. He trusted no man with an accent. He had tossed Lombrado out into the street, and Lombrado had hurried away in silence, his face swollen and bloody, his head down as he went up the street, ignoring the curious passers-by who stared at his blood-spattered shirt and jacket.

Two weeks later a messenger brought

Dicks a message. Would he care to come to the Pantucci house on Charlton Street, take a glass of wine, sit down and quietly discuss a business proposition? He checked the reactions of some of his other patrons: the politician, who was Irish, and the brothelkeeper, who despite his nickname was German. He asked a couple of others, just to take a sounding. Nobody knew anything about Pantucci. Everyone figured it would be a good idea to find out what the Italians were up to, without committing himself.

He went and he listened with growing impatience to the droning old goat in his wickerwork chair. You could not fault this Pantucci on old-world courtesy, or on the quality of his wine; but he took the best part of an hour to get around to his proposition, and by that time Georgie Dicks wasn't even bothering to keep the boredom off his face. In the end, he cut the old man's drone off by standing up abruptly, telling Pantucci he just plain hadn't got the time to waste listening to his reminiscences of the old days in Sicily. As he understood it, Don Gabriele was offering him a deal. Well, he didn't make deals, not with anyone, and especially not with dagos. He remembered the stunned look of shock on the still-swollen face of Lombrado as he'd stalked out of the house, more than satisfied with his handling of the old man.

His satisfaction hadn't lasted long.

Three nights later, as he was walking home from the station house, he was very quietly taken off the street and into a building on Macdougal Street, and efficiently bound with wire after having been stripped of his clothing. He never saw the faces of the three men, although he always suspected that one of them was Lombrado. He was in the house for three hours, and when they turned him loose he was as empty as a drum. Without so much as a blow, without having broken his skin in a single place, the trio convinced Captain George Dicks that it would be very much in his own best interests to accept the generous offer which Don Gabriele Pantucci was making to him, an offer which, he would understand, would not be repeated should he make the mistake of talking about it either to his Irish politician friend, or his German brothelkeeper friend, or anyone else.

Georgie Dicks never spoke of what had happened to him in that house, never would. But he still woke sometimes with the sighing birth of a scream in his throat, sweat drenching his pyjamas when he thought of the flat blades of the knives touching his scrotum, and the expressionless disinterest in the eyes of the three masked men. They had made him scream, they had made him thrash, sweating, his body voiding itself in abject fear as they made him face the one thing about himself that he had never wanted, never needed to face, the one thing he had probably always known deep inside himself: that he was, before all else, an abject, craven coward. Had they hurt him, had they really used the knives on him, it might have been bearable. It was the threat, and only the threat, which destroyed him.

Time passed. Outwardly, Captain Dicks ran his precinct with the same efficiency and correctness he'd always displayed. His arrest-books were always full enough but never padded. His men were always roughly where they should be roughly when they were supposed to be. There wasn't too suspiciously much spit-and-polish on parades, but there wasn't any sloppiness either. His sergeants ran the station house well, and Dicks kept what he called a 'weather eye' on policy and the major cases in which the Fifth Precinct had an interest. Plus his other briefs, of course. There was a new 'Vice Squad' up at Mulberry Street which was given to making unannounced raids on what the newspapers had taken to calling dens of iniquity, and he had to check regularly to make sure none of his clients was on their list. Once in a while he received a request in a plain manilla envelope from his friend at Tammany, and had things to organize. His third responsibility and — truth told and shame the Devil — his most important, was to keep Don Gabriele informed. He took this responsibility more seriously than any other, although at no time had Don

Gabriele ever spoken a name he must watch for, an address to be safeguarded, a man who must be protected. *Cose Italiani*, the old man had nodded, smiling. 'You know what I mean. Anything to do with us Italians.'

He really meant *anything*, too. So, maybe twice a week, Dicks would drop into a restaurant or a café, or take a beer with some faceless young Italian. He never grew to like any of them any better, but he learned how to live with it. Once in a while he'd take a walk in the Park, or accept a lift from someone in a closed carriage. If anything really urgent came up, he had a telephone number to call. He'd checked it out, of course: a small letterpress printing shop on lower Broadway run by a gnomish Italian called Agguato, who had no police blotter and led a blameless life. Nothing there he could one day use, so he'd sat back and watched the two hundred dollars being paid each month into the bank account he'd opened at Don Gabriele's suggestion in the name of Richard George.

He got the call from Joe Petrosino

about six o'clock.

'Hello, Petrosino,' Dicks said. He knew the head of the Italian Branch and, like most of the precinct captains, he didn't like him, had enjoyed his recent fall from grace.

'George, hello George, you there? Listen, I want you to pick someone up for me. Can you do it?'

'Sure,' Dicks said. 'Anyone we know?'

'Name of Petto, Tommaso Petto,' Petrosino said. 'He usually hangs out at that place on the right-hand side of Elizabeth Street, the one on the corner of Hester, know the one I mean?'

'I know it,' Dicks said, offended at being asked whether he knew the name of a saloon on his own patch. 'The Mediterraneo.'

'That's the one,' Petrosino said. 'That is what I want you to do, George. Pick up Petto. Don't scare him off, for God's sake! If he's wearing a gold-plated hunter watch, get it sent up here to me as fast as you can, will you?'

'And if he's not?'

'I think he will be,' Petrosino said.

'Anyway, pick him up.'

'You sending a warrant down?'

'Right now,' the detective said. 'After you send the watch up here, hold Petto incommunicado till I get back. I got to go to Buffalo.'

'You sound awful sure he'll have this watch,' Dicks said dubiously.

'I am,' Petrosino said. 'Get on with it, please, George.'

Dicks' anger rose like a tide. Petrosino hadn't been on the horn two minutes, and already he was making hurry-up noises. He always had been a hard-nosed son of a bitch.

'I'll get at it,' he growled, 'as soon as I can. We only do miracles for the Mayor, you know.'

'I know,' Petrosino said, missing both Dicks's anger and his irony. 'Uh, listen, you'd better send a couple of the heavy mob down there to pick Petto up. Last time he was arrested, he damn near tore the arm off of one of the patrolmen.'

'I'll keep it in mind,' Dicks said. 'You wouldn't maybe have a description up there, too, would you?'

'Naturally,' Petrosino said, missing Dicks's sarcasm and injecting a little stiffness into his own voice. Did the fool think he'd ask him to arrest someone without giving him a description? 'I'll send it down with the warrant right now.'

'Well, thanks,' Dicks said.

'Welcome,' Petrosino said. 'Call me back as soon as you pick him up, okay?'

He had hung up before Dicks could snap out the scathing reply he had formulated, something along the lines of what the hell did Petrosino think the Fifth Precinct was, his own fucking private fucking army? Did he think that all he had to do was pick up the goddamned telephone and everyone down here dropped his britches and galloped out doing the bidding of Lieutenant fucking Petrosino? He slammed the flat of his hand down on his blotter. That Petrosino!

After a while he heard a knock on his door and the desk sergeant came in with an envelope. He slit it open with the silver letter-knife which had been the gift of a grateful market-stall owner and slid out the warrant for the arrest of Tommaso 'the Bull' Petto in connexion with the murder of Benedetto Madonnia. Jesus! he thought, that one. He read the description of Petto, and then reached for the telephone. Before he could touch it, however, it rang, and he heard the familiar voice of Lombrado at the other end. 'I'm glad you called,' he said breathlessly. 'I was just going to call you.'

'What about?' Lombrado asked.

'I just got a warrant sent down here for me to pick up — '

'Tommaso Petto. I know,' Lombrado said silkily.

'You — how the hell — ?'

'Never mind that,' Lombrado said. 'It is important that you do exactly as I tell you. Do you understand?'

'Sure,' Dicks said, 'but what — ?'

'Listen,' Lombrado snapped impatiently, 'Sit still and listen!'

For ten minutes George Dicks sat in his chair as Antonio Lombrado told him exactly what he had to do and exactly how he had to do it. No aspect of the matter seemed to have been overlooked, no detail so small that Lombrado did not cover it. Eventually he was finished. 'You understand exactly what you have to do?' he asked.

'Sure,' Dicks said. 'I understand.'

'Then do it,' Lombrado said and hung up, leaving George Dicks, Captain, staring at the humming earpiece.

The fix was in.

★　★　★

Don Vito left Manhattan that same night.

It was not a flight — far from it. He had been planning a trip to New Orleans for some months to visit the son of his good friend in Palermo, Antonio Passananti. The threat of intra-family war was gone, and the well-oiled machine he had — as he liked to think of it — repaired was again humming like a good sewing-machine. From New Orleans he planned — although he had not revealed his intentions to anyone other than his confidant, Lombrado — to make a return trip to Palermo. He felt that the trip was sagaciously timed. By going, he would remove the target which the Federal investigators were so assiduously seeking, leaving them a hydra with many heads which they could not combat. In going, Fate had delivered him an opportunity to remove from the paw of his friends the thorn which had so long plagued them, the policeman Petrosino. The man was dogged, and he had influence in some high places which would be better diverted. It would be a pleasant thing to leave behind as his memorial.

Don Vito had been in America for a long time. Too long, he felt. He missed the blossoms on the trees and the harsh sun of his homeland. He missed the leisurely pace of his old life, and there were things at home to which he must eventually, inescapably, attend.

He would stay a while in New Orleans, he thought. Then a boat to Genoa, another to Naples, and the *piroscafo* from there to Palermo.

It would be good to see Sicily again.

12

In a way, Flynn thought, it had been funny.

If you wrote it down as a comedy, put some good lines in, it would be funny; it would make people laugh. He shrugged: expecting Petrosino to not jump in with both feet was like asking a fighting bull kindly not to charge when the matador waves his cape.

He walked down West 42nd Street, past the sleazy arcades with their shrill come-ons for the merchant sailors fresh out of the docks, the sun in his eyes and a cold breeze coming up off the river. He shrugged his overcoat closer around his shoulders, bowing his head and narrowing his eyes against the cutting edge of the wind. You'd just know that Joe Petrosino was going to choose February to sail, that he'd pick the coldest, cruellest, most callous month of the year to set forth on his investigative trip to Italy. You'd just know, Flynn thought resignedly, that when he'd phoned to ask would it be okay to come down to the ship to say 'so long', Petrosino had replied off-handedly that he could if he liked.

He was sure back of the line when they handed the charm out, Flynn thought. So why was he shlepping across Manhattan to bid him a fond farewell?

Well, for one thing, Petrosino had had a hard time. Finally, totally, made to look like a complete and utter charlatan. He'd claimed, of course, that it was a Mafia plot to discredit him, but, with the best intentions in the world, even Flynn coudn't imagine that the Mafia cared that much about Joe Petrosino. What had cooked Petrosino's goose was not so much a Mafia conspiracy as a good old-fashioned all-American foul-up. And you never saw goose better cooked. Any time, any place.

In a way it had been sort of funny. Petrosino had sent orders to the Fifth Precinct to pick up Tommaso Petto and they'd gone out and scoured the streets for him, five burly patrolmen with their muscles showing all over their heads, truncheons drawn and pistol holsters unfastened. Tommaso the Bull was reputed to be a tough one who'd kicked up a hell of a fight the last time he'd been pulled in, so they were taking no chances this time. If he so much as blinked, they'd break his skull. They learned that he was in the Meditteraneo — apparently he nearly always was after six in the evening, taking a drink of wine and playing cards with his cronies — and they went in there like a Kansas twister to get him. Dander up, ready for anything, five of New York's finest thundered across the saloon like stampeding African elephants and the whole goddamned table, bottles, cards, and innocent bystanders went over like it had been bombed. Several of those who'd been knocked to the floor in this unannounced attack took umbrage and tried to see how many different kinds of lump their fists, chair legs, bottles and sundry other weapons could raise on the heads of the five policemen. The cops returned the compliment in spades, and for a while it was one of the best scraps that they'd seen in the quarter for anything up to a week. When the smoke cleared, there were two cops unconscious in the rubble, sprawled between or under half a dozen miscellaneous bystanders in various stages of coherency. The other three patrolmen put the arm on Tommaso 'the Bull' Petto, easily recognizable from Petrosino's description and his gold-plated hunter watch. To their considerable surprise, the hulking Italian, who looked every inch his nickname, came along so quietly that by the time they got him to the station house they were jocularly referring to him as Ferdinand. It was downright disgusting, the way they'd got themselves all fired up for a scrap, but there you were.

The desk sergeant charged Petto, relieved him of the contents of his pockets, asked him if he had anything to say, Petto, glowering like some live incarnation of the proverbial brick out-house, shook his heavy head.

'You got the wrong man,' he said in Italian.

'Howzat?' the desk sergeant said.

'I'm not Petto,' the prisoner said. 'You got the wrong man.'

'Anyone here speak this lingo?' the sergeant shouted.

'You kidding?' someone shouted back.

'Oh, thanks,' said the desk sergeant sourly.

'Your name's Petto, right?' he said to the prisoner.

'No,' the man said. 'You got the wrong man.'

'Don't you know any English, Tommaso?'

'Not me,' the prisoner said in English.

'Sure,' the sergeant said, soothingly. He held up the goldplated watch. 'An' this is a family heirloom, right?'

'You got the wrong man,' said the prisoner in Italian. It was the only thing he said to anyone, no matter what the question.

'You want some coffee, Tommaso?'

'You got the wrong man.'

'You want us to phone someone, Petto. Your lawyer, maybe?'

'You got the wrong man.'

In the end, they just plain gave up on

him and shoved him in the tank to tell the drunks and vags that he wasn't the right man, while someone ran the gold-plated hunter watch up to Joe Petrosino at Mulberry Street. He was off ten minutes later like a hare with its tail on fire. Next morning he telegraphed Police Headquarters from Buffalo:

WATCH IDENTIFIED BY GRAZIELLA MADONNIA AS BELONGING TO HER HUSBAND BENEDETTO STOP ARRAIGN PETTO SOONEST FOR TRIAL CHARGE MURDER ONE RETURNING IMMEDIATELY STOP
                    PETROSINO

Both feet, Flynn thought.

He cannoned off the shoulder of a man hurrying in the opposite direction and apologized, realizing as he did that he was wasting his breath. No matter how long he lived in New York he'd never get used to the fact that nobody had time for common-or-garden courtesies on the street. If you fell dying, people tended to step around you. Or on you, he thought

305

with a grim grin. In New York, everybody hustled. Being first was what mattered, not being nice. Everybody hustled. Like the newspaper reporters.

They always kept someone hanging around the station houses, keeping an eye on the drunk tanks, in case anyone 'known' was wheeled in. There was always room for one of those 'Banker spends night in Fifth Precinct drunk tank' stories, guaranteed to give the readers of the yellow press a moment's *frisson* over their morning coffee, confirming their suspicions that bankers, for all their frosty uppityness, were no better than anyone else. The fact that the stories sometimes ruined the lives of said bankers was neither here nor there. Reporters weren't paid to protect the private lives of bankers. Everybody hustled, right? Like the reporter on the night-beat at the Fifth Precinct.

Frankly, he couldn't have been interested in a blue-chinned thug like Tommaso 'the Bull' Petto. You saw that kind all the time down here: a cheap strong-arm man, a saloon bouncer, maybe, or a dance-hall chucker-out, or even the 'bodyguard' of some tremulous pander. He hardly even heard the charge; but he did hear the name of Benedetto Madonnia, and he sat up in the scarred wooden chair he'd been sprawled across as if someone had connected live electrical terminals to his backside. This might not just be some dreary night court story. This might be a scoop; he might get a by-line; he might even be able to swing that job on the *Trib* on the strength of this!

Concealing his excitement as best he could, he wandered across to where the desk-sergeant was standing, a mug of muddy coffee cradled in his heavy hands. He knew him: Pete something.

'That Petto, Pete,' he said off-handedly. 'Whose bust is it?'

Sergeant Peter Watts made an expression of disgust and told the reporter what he had been instructed to say by Captain Dicks: that all credit for Petto's arrest, and all inquiries about it, should be directed to Lieutenant Petrosino of the Italian Branch. It was, he said, a part of a much bigger case involving criminal conspiracy on a large scale and Lieutenant Petrosino was confident that it would lead to the smashing of an organized ring of Italian criminals operating in the quarter. When Georgie Dicks had told his sergeants all this, they'd listened to him with mounting amazement. *Noblesse* of such magnitude was scarcely typical of their captain, and his intense mien as he told them to be sure that no one attempted to steal any of Petrosino's laurels had been something to behold.

However, it was no skin off their noses if the Old Man had gone daft in his old age, so Watts told the reporter the story straight. The reporter phoned his news editor and the news editor turned out the files from the morgue and they had the most beautiful front page you've ever seen in your life, the whole *shmeer* about how the out-of-favour but ever-diligent Lieutenant Petrosino had finally broken the case which had for so long remained outstanding on the books of the New York Police Department. The story was compounded of about nine parts guesswork to one part hypothesis, but backed up by the morgue stuff on Madonnia, some of the juicier pics, all those lovely innuendoes about which particular part of his body had been found stuffed in his mouth — *saorists!* If this didn't sell an extra fifty thousand, the news editor told himself when he saw the first pull, damned if he knew what would! By the time it hit the street, Petrosino would be arriving at Grand Central, and every paper in town would be there to get his statement, trying for some kind of exclusive. But the *Post* would have the beat. 'Let 'er go!' he said to the printing room boss, and made a mental note to see the boss the following day about that rise he'd been promised.

★ ★ ★

By the time you crossed Eighth Avenue, you were deep into what they now called Hell's Kitchen. Actually, it wasn't too bad in the daytime, although you still had to watch yourself. There were still plenty of street jackals in the empty hallways of the peeling tenements whose decaying frontage lined the street. Over on this side of town lay all the sweat-shops, all the mass-labour joints, Blake's dark satanic mills come to life with a vengence. HIGGINS CARPET FACTORY, a huge sign blared, in letters painted ten feet high, on the blank brick face of a factory wall overlooking the avenue. JOHNSON'S ORGAN WORKS, shouted another. 'Glad to hear it,' Flynn muttered, hurrying along across town.

Up on Eleventh Avenue, he could see the smoke billowing from the chimney of the Metropolitan Gas Company, and further uptown, the hulking squat shape of the Municipal Oxygen Gasworks. There was a constant tremor of noise borne in the air now, a noise of humming and roaring and singing and clattering and vibrating and jangling machinery joined into an almost physical presence that pressed on the eardrums like someone's palm. It was the veritable sound of the twentieth century, the sound of piano factories making pianos, iron foundries making iron, printing works, candy manufacturers, carriage builders, ornamental ironworks, lime kilns, stone-masons, fisheries, sawmills, shipyards and dockside cranes, intermingling with the sound of the voices and the throb of the bodies of the immigrant horde who operated the machines, sweated in the factories, oiled the machines they cursed, cursed the machines they oiled; the thousand after thousand thousand who toiled morning, noon, and night in these echoing mausoleums of industry, before staggering home to the desolated tene-ments where they slept and ate and made love and raised kids and eventually died forgotten. The streets were packed, thronged with delivery drays and push-carts, horse-buggies, streetcars, railway carriages, waggons, street vendors of every kind and every size, kids running everywhere, most of them in rags. Men stood quiet and still on the corners of streets, leaning against the walls and watching, only their eyes moving, seeing everything, weighing possibilities. They weighed Flynn as coldly and objectively as they weighed everything else, a possibility to be judged, thought over, and finally discarded.

He hurried on.

He could see the North River up at the end of the slightly rising street, a raft of logs out in midstream being ferried down to the mills at 40th Street. The tall masts of ocean-going ships poked up at the unfriendly sky. Poor Petrosino, Flynn thought. He'd fallen for the whole damned thing, borne the entire brunt of what followed.

The papers had found out what train he was coming back on from Buffalo and every one of them had a man up at Grand Central when he stepped off on to the platform. He'd seen the paper already, and, being Petrosino, he wasn't about to miss his moment of glory.

Petrosino had his *coup*.

He'd brought off the trick that would refurbish his tarnished image with the Commissioners. Just as he'd proved that the Italian Branch wasn't run by a crackpot, conspiracy-obsessed nut. Here, as a result of investigative work of which the NYPD could be proud, was proof of what he had always said, proof that the

Italian syndicate did exist. Now, surely, the State Legislature must give him the funds and the staff to stamp it out once and for all. Oh, boy, he gave it to them, Flynn remembered, seeing again the crowd on the windswept platform in the echoing glass-roofed station. The boys couldn't wait to get downtown and set it up in 96-point caps. He'd watched Petrosino swelling visibly as he shouted answers to the questions the reporters threw at him, waiting, vainly of course, for Petrosino to even hint that the lead from which all this had stemmed had been provided by the Department of Justice, that his supreme moment of glory had come from a lead supplied by his good friend and colleague William J Flynn. No chance. This was Joe Petrosino's day and he wasn't about to share it with anyone.

He got his headlines, by God! He got his picture on the front page of every newspaper in town. Hero, they called him. Brilliant! Dogged! Indefatigable! The Nemesis of Organized Crime! Petrosino!

Who'll clean up New York?

Petrosino!

Who'll root out corruption, without mercy?

Petrosino!

Who's a shoo-in to be our next Chief of Police? — Now, hold on a minute there, boys!

No, no, Petrosino!

Flynn came to a halt at the gateway to Pier 83. The wind was really biting now, buffeting him as he stood there, one hand holding the lapels of his overcoat together, the other clutching his hat. The edge of the wind made his eyes water. There she was: the *Duke of Genoa*, flying the Italian flag, the American flag, and some bunting. Cabin Fourteen, he reminded himself, and ask for Signor Simone Velletri, commercial traveller, and not Lieutenant Petrosino, Nemesis of Organized Crime. Petrosino was making this trip incognito. Whether the secrecy was, as Petrosino said, so that the Mafia would not get word of his intended investigation or, as scuttlebutt had it at Mulberry Street, because Petrosino had been told to get the hell out of Manhattan any way he liked as long as it was quietly, Flynn didn't know.

At three the ship would sail, taking Petrosino on his 'top secret' assignment to Rome, Naples, and Palermo, where he would investigate the roots of the Mafia, assemble dossiers on criminals who had emigrated to America without declaring their criminal past, unearth the evidence which, once and for all, would break the stranglehold of the *alianza*. Flynn remembered having to control his jaw, which had begun to drop when Petrosino had insisted — insisted! — that there be no publicity about his trip, no farewell parties, no Press, nothing. He did not want the *mafiosi* tipped off that he was coming. If he saw the look which passed between the Commissioner, the Chief and the Mayor, he didn't react to it, which was strange, because it plainly said 'Humour him.' Everyone had had more than enough of Petrosino's name in the newspapers, thank you. He'd had all the publicity anyone could want, and by God! let everyone fervently hope he never got any more.

The man who had been arrested was not Tommaso Petto.

It went the whole damned way to court. Petrosino, of course, never went downtown to see Petto. He'd see him in court. He didn't know him to look at worth spit, anyway. So Petto — that is to say, the man they thought was Petto — was wheeled in front of the judge at the Criminal Court for formal arraignment. The judge had got all the way up to where he was about to send 'Petto' for trial when Paul le Barbier had risen from his seat and proceeded to cut Lieutenant Joseph Petrosino into tiny, flayed, bloody strips in front of the entire City and State of New York. The prisoner's name was Giovanni Pecoraro.

He said — through an interpreter — that he had tried to tell anyone who would listen that he was not Tommaso Petto, but they had not understood him. No one to whom he had spoken understood Italian, nor had any attempt been made to find someone who did. He said this looking directly, as he had been instructed by Paul le Barbier, at Joe

Petrosino. After Pecoraro had spoken, le Barbier got to his feet and proceeded to produce all the documents ever registered to prove that Pecoraro was indeed who he said he was, a good Italian boy who loved his parents and his wife and their children, and who could produce as many character witnesses as the Court might desire who would swear to Pecoraro's unblemished character, his blameless life, his nigh-angelic goodness. Paul le Barbier had been superb, Flynn recalled. He did practically everything except recite the Declaration of Independence, and when he was finished Petrosino looked as if someone had just pumped all the blood out of his body.

The papers crucified him, of course. That night, next morning, next evening. Extra! Extra! Read all about it! They forgot everything good Petrosino had ever done. Forgot his sometime successes. Forgot that he had indeed warned McKinley that an attempt was to be made on his life. Forgot — no, dismissed — the thousand occasions on which Petrosino had risked his life in the dark alleys of Little Italy. And in forgetting all this, forgot the most important thing of all, the very thing which Petrosino had sworn to fight: the *alianza* itself. Of course, Petrosino was a much easier mark to hit, and everyone had witnessed his mistake.

It took practically no time for City Hall to get itself off the hook. Lieutenant Petrosino was given sick leave, and a release was issued saying he had broken down due to overwork and would be away for some time. Meanwhile, various confidential reports flew back and forth. Flynn saw some of them, 'confidential' being a flexible condition in the New York Police Department, and knew what was coming, tried to prepare Petrosino for it. He wasn't listening.

When they finally called him in and gave him the face-saver, he grabbed it and if you hadn't been looking for the deadness behind the eyes, you'd have thought it was the old Petrosino back again. Flynn knew it was a pose, but he didn't know how to let Petrosino know he knew. Maybe in the end he'd have to go along with the pretence like the rest of them.

What happened was really very simple, politically speaking. The Governor had been getting mightily sick and tired of Petrosino's constant interference in matters which were none of his concern, writing to Congressmen and Senators, encouraging President Roosevelt to breathe down his, the Governor's, neck with questions about why Petrosino wasn't being given the money he wanted, the office space he needed, the extra men he had to have to combat organized crime. Up at Albany, in a room heavy with cigar-smoke, they concluded that they didn't like having the heavy hand of the Washington political factory on their shoulders, mucking about with what were strictly New York matters. A pox on Washington! They didn't like Washington at best. And what they especially didn't like was Lieutenant Joseph Petrosino. Now when the boys up at Albany decide they don't like something or somebody, stand back! Someone tossed Petrosino's outline proposal for an investigative trip to Italy on the table and said it was a way out.

'How?' asked the Governor.

'Give him the money and let him get lost,' was the reply. 'He'll be gone for six months. By the time he gets back all this will have blown over. He'll be forgotten.'

There were grave nods around the polished oak table. The City and State of New York wanted Joe Petrosino out of its hair for as long as that could be arranged. Let him go screw up the goddamned Eye-talians.

Done, done, and done. The Governor asked for a budget proposal and got one within an hour. The vote to permit Petrosino's trip to Italy was unanimous. He was summoned to the Mayor's office on 29 January. Now, on 9 February, he was aboard the *Duke of Genoa* and ready to sail. With a long sigh, Bill Flynn started across the cobblestoned dock road and down the quayside. He knew he'd be the only one who'd come down to the ship to say good-bye to Petrosino. He also knew that Petrosino wouldn't thank him for coming. He could almost predict the conversation.

'Just came down to wish you *bon voyage*, Joe,' he'd say.

'Oh,' Petrosino would reply. 'You needn't have bothered.'

He grinned and went up the gang-plank. Trouble with you, Flynn, he told himself, is you're too damned touchy.

13

The ship's engines started up.

He could feel the deck tremble with the surge of power that came vibrating up from the engine room, and then heard the thundering rush of churned water at the stern as the screws bit deep below the surface. He leaned against the rail, sheltered from the buffeting wind by a lifeboat, and watched the busy scene on the pier below. A man shouted something, cupping his hands at each side of his mouth, but the words were snatched away in the breeze. Gulls glou-glou'ed as they circled the boiling wake, hoping for a titbit churned from the bottom.

The dockside slid slowly backwards, giving the impression that it was moving, and not the ship, until you looked away and saw the boat was edging out towards open water. Then the pilot signalled for full power and pointed the noisy *piroscafo* southwest across the *Bacino di Piliero* and out into the Bay of Naples.

Joe Petrosino stood by the rail looking back. He could see the whole city spread across the hook of land behind him: the heavy walls of the old fortifications at sea level, and behind them the warren of buildings climbing to the left and then back right to the top of Vomero, crowned by its monastery. Off to the left lay Santa Lucia, behind the Borgo Marinaro. Down along the sweeping reach of the bay, Vesuvio wisped smoke into the clear, crisp air. He wished for a fleeting moment that he had taken the time to go to Pompeii, Herculaneum, Capri: all the places he had heard about all his life, the legends of his own past, dream places implanted in his mind years back by his parents in America.

All those years, he thought.

He wondered if they'd be proud of him, their son Giuseppe, if they could see him now, prosperous-looking, well-dressed, leaning on the rail of a steamship heading for Palermo; Tenente Petrosino of the New York Police, respected, perhaps even famous, smiling a little as he saw the twin peaks of Capri poke up over the horizon.

He had been welcomed in Rome. In Naples, he had been feted. Everyone had heard of him here. He was almost a legend, a folk-hero, one of their own who had really made good in the New World, the fabulous land of America. They knew nothing of the events which had preceded Petrosino's arrival in Italy, he did not tell them.

To be truthful, the sense of failure which had touched him in the weeks before he had left New York had evaporated to be replaced by a stolid determination that, in the end, he would prevail. And so he worked; by God how he worked!

Time and again, Commissioner Longobardi, who'd been seconded to give him every assistance he needed in the Eternal City, had thrown up his hands in astonishment, amazement, sometimes even disgust, at the pace Petrosino had set. He was a shallow, slighty built man of perhaps forty-five or fifty, who wore a dark blue suit and a dark blue shirt and black shoes every day of the week except Sunday, when he wore a white shirt to go to Mass.

'Giuseppe,' Longobardi had reproached him. 'Life is not all work, my friend. There is time for other things. Once in a while, a little pleasure, a little relaxation.'

Petrosino had shaken his head. 'I'm not here for pleasure, Luigi,' he'd said. Not once, but many times. 'Many people depend on me. What I discover here may have a profound effect on American justice.'

He believed it; and, of course, the conviction in his voice convinced everyone he spoke to. Why else would the American Government send such an important figure so far?

'Of course, of course,' Longobardi would say, soothingly. 'But to take a decent meal, drink a glass of wine on the Via Veneto, you should also make time for these things, too. To come so far and not — '

'Luigi,' Petrosino would say, patiently but impatient, 'I don't have the time.'

If it offended Longobardi, and he

sometimes had the feeling that the Italian police chief was put out by his refusals, well, he just had to live with perhaps being less popular than would otherwise have been the case. It would be nice to play the prodigal son, but there was just too damned much to be done. He was being subsidized by the taxpayer and it was his duty to waste neither time nor money. As a civil servant himself, Longobardi ought to understand that better than anyone. Finally, though, the Italian had won, and insisted that on Petrosino's last night in Rome they relax. They took a carriage out to the villa Borghese for coffee, followed by a look at the Colosseum and the tumbled puzzle of the Forum. Even this early in the year, the evening was balmy, the streets speckled with leisurely pedestrians. Longobardi insisted that Petrosino at least see San Pietro, and they clattered across the Tiber, over the Ponte San Angelo, Longobardi chattering away about the statues and the castles while Petrosino nodded, his mind on the information he was unearthing from the dossiers in

Police Headquarters, masses and masses of it, copying in his sloping scrawl until his hand would function no more, taking bundles more back each night to the Hotel d'Inghilterra, to study until his eyes moved in their sockets reluctantly, as though they might squeak with fatigue; until he fell into dreamless unconsciousness with the papers scattered over the bedspread.

He was always first to arrive at the squat yellow building which housed the Police Department, tapping his feet impatiently until he could really get started. Walking from his hotel, his mind was too full to see the crowded, colourful streets, too preoccupied to notice the barrows with their blocks of ice covered with blood-red watermelon or ice-cream. He walked head down, engrossed in what he was doing, noticing only that the sewer covers were embossed SPQR, his mind on the revelations in the documents he was examining, immersed in his own role as undercover nemesis of the Mafia. Perhaps he realized that he was indulging his own theatricality, but he told himself it was just a little, only a tiny bit. He hardly ever thought of New York, except as a place to which he must inevitably return. He would only go back in triumph. Anyway, the acting was acceptable here in Rome: they were all vain, all *poseurs*, promenading upon the stage of their own existence. He was glad there was only a little of that in his own make-up.

Well, Rome was behind him now. He'd tossed his coin into the Fontana di Trevi, paid his hotel bill — six lire a night — and taken the *rapido* to Naples, *il paese natale*. He loved it, loved the whole city from the moment he came out of the station into the Piazza Garibaldi. He had only a few days, and much to do, but here he revelled in the atavistic feeling of having always known this place, with its belled mules waiting at the refreshment kiosks, its hurdy-gurdies and the strings of lemons in the shops, the street vendors selling glow-worms and tortoises, the shoeshine boys with their ornate footstools. Now Naples was behind him, too.

The steamship was well out into the

Mediterranean, pointing her blunt bows down the curve of the world towards Sicily, towards Palermo, towards what he knew would be the climax of his quest. For it was in Sicily, in Messina and Palermo and Syracuse, that he would find the hardest information. The dossiers he had copied in their hundreds in Rome and Naples, these were valuable; no, invaluable. They were already on their way back to Commissioner Bingham in New York, to Flynn at the Department of Justice. They would all be vetted, taken apart, cross-indexed, checked out, filed. They would provide the basis of a complete record of known criminals of Italian descent now living in America, especially those known to have or have had Mafia, Black Hand, or Camorra connexions. He had not even had time to send postcards. To tell the truth, he could only think of one person to send a postcard to: Bill Flynn. He'd bought a pretty card, a little garish in its hand-tinting, but showing the whole bay. He decided to write it when he got to Palermo.

The Italian police had been more than co-operative. No trouble had been too great, no request too arcane. He touched his breast pocket, reassured by the soft crackle of paper. He had letters of introduction from the Chief of Police of Rome, the American Ambassador, the Chief of Carabinieri in Naples, the Secretary of the Minister of the Interior, all requesting, in the name of the Government of Italy, that Tenente Giuseppe Petrosino of New York be rendered the utmost co-operation, the fullest possible assistance, and the most complete secrecy. Petrosino left the rail, watching Capri fade on the horizon in the ship's wake, pacing vigorously along the deck, face ruddied by the crisp breeze.

Palermo, he thought.

14

Daily, at around eleven in the morning, work in Palermo comes slowly to a stop. Some people say that this habit is a throwback to Moorish times a thousand years before the Normans came to plunge Sicily into the black pit of feudal night. Others, perhaps more worldly-wise, will tell you that it has grown out of the pleasure of the men in the darkly discreet clothes whom you will see in certain crowded cafés near the Quattro Canti, standing close together with just enough room to raise the tiny cups of *caffe solo* to unsmiling lips, talking in quiet voices beside the zinc-topped serving bars; cool and guarded men, watching nothing and seeing everything. But whether it be the preference of *mafiosi* or the pleasure of Sultans matters ultimately not at all, for the tradition, like all Sicilian traditions, is old-established and inimical to change. So, at around eleven each morning, the streets are redolent of fresh-ground coffee, and people move without haste in the sharp black shadows of the pink buildings, freed for a short while from whatever cares beset them.

Michele Ferrantelli was such a one, sitting comfortably in the carriage which had been sent for him by Don Vito Cascio Ferro, on his way to the big house on the Via Archirafi where he would celebrate his recent election to the position of Deputy for Palermo over a leisurely lunch with the man to whom he owed his election. There was no doubt of that, Ferrantelli told himself as the horse clip-clopped up the Via Roma. Every square foot of wall-space in Palermo had been covered with posters showing his smiling portrait and the legend in huge letters bidding the good citizens of Palermo to vote for him, 'l'amico del Popolo' — which every good citizen well knew translated as 'the friend of the friends.' His election had been a walk-over, a matter of course. The campaign had not cost him a *lire*, which was just as well, for Michele Ferrantelli was not a rich man. Don Vito Cascio Ferro's friendship was worth more than riches, however, and his support had made the contest between himself and Rafaele Palizzolo something of a one-horse race.

He arrived at the Ferro house at eleven forty-five, and was met by an unsmiling servant who asked him to wait on the patio. Don Vito, the man explained, had been detained by some urgent business in Palermo, but would be home and join Don Michele for luncheon as soon as possible. Perhaps, in the meantime, Don Michele would care for something to drink, a glass of wine, perhaps, or an aperitif? Flattered by the attention, and by being addressed as a don by those who served the real Don, Michele Ferrantelli chose a comfortable wicker chair in the warmest corner of the conservatory, where he could sit and look out across the bay. It was a bright sunny day, pleasantly warm there among the rubbery-leaved plants and cacti. The sea was ultramarine, and millions of flecks of light danced on its surface. Seabirds wheeled and dived over the cliffs of Monte Pellegrino.

Michele Ferrantelli checked his watch; it was almost exactly noon. Idly, he sipped his wine and wondered where Don Vito was. He would have been astonished, appalled, to know that at that precise moment Vito Cascio Ferro was standing in the shadow of a huge palm on the Piazza Marina, his right hand clenched around the butt of the heavy Lebel revolver in his pocket, his narrowed eyes fixed on the burly figure of Joseph Petrosino hurrying across the square to meet him.

★ ★ ★

Don Vito was informed of every step the American took. From the moment Petrosino stepped off the boat on the morning of 28 February 1909, until the moment of the meeting in the Piazza Marina, nothing he did escaped the eyes of the *amici*. The driver of the carriage which brought him the short distance from the port to the Hotel de France, in the square dominated by the splendid Garibaldi Garden and its exotic shrubs and trees, passed the word along, as did the *portiere* who took Petrosino's bags up to Room Sixteen — five lire a night — and the desk clerk who added the news that Petrosino had registered under the name Simone Valenti.

At first this puzzled Passananti, who was co-ordinating the flow of information; puzzled him, that is, until he decided that Petrosino intended to play 'secret agent' to the hilt, whether the news of his mission had been made public or not. It was only later that he came to the conclusion the American did not know that the news of his intentions had been published in the newspapers.

The manager of the Banca Commerciale told Passananti's men that Petrosino had used his real name to open an account — 2000 lire — and arranged for any mail to be addressed to him in care of the bank. He swore the manager of the bank, whose name was Umberto Bianchi, to utmost secrecy. After this, Petrosino went to visit the office of William A Bishop, the American consul, in the Piazza Castelnuovo. What transpired there the *amici* did not know, but it was not difficult to guess: Bishop had been enrolled to assist Petrosino in his work. And so it proved.

Bishop made several calls to officials in the Ministries and Government offices, asking for their assistance and co-operation. Petrosino was particularly interested in going through the records of criminal convictions held at the offices of the Tribunale. He remained there most of the day, emerging just before six and going to the store of Alfredo Capra in the Via Roma, where he paid a month's rental on a Remington portable typewriter, using the name Salvatore Basilico. He took the machine to his room at the Hotel de France, where he wrote some letters which he brought down and asked the desk clerk to post. One was to Commissioner of Police Bingham in New York. One was to his brother Vincenzo in Padula, near Salerno. Both letters were steamed open and read. Neither contained anything of interest: they merely stated that Petrosino had arrived safely and was looking forward to what lay ahead, and that mail could be sent to him in care of the Banca Commerciale. At eight thirty that evening, Petrosino came out into the piazza and walked across to the Caffe Oreto on the corner next to the streetcar terminus. He sat alone at a corner table looking miserable. He blew his nose constantly into a large handkerchief. The waiter told Passananti's people that Petrosino said he'd caught a cold on the boat. Around nine fifteen, he got up and paid his bill — Lire 2.70 — and walked back to his hotel. By ten he was asleep. From this quickly established routine, Petrosino deviated not one iota during the next five days, unless you could count slightly earlier quitting of the Tribunale building, slightly earlier arrival at his hotel, slightly longer on the Remington as he copied out the notes which he had taken during the long day's examination of the records there.

Had he done no more, what followed inevitably might have been avoided; but he was Petrosino and not only did he know no fear, he did not have the sense to realize his danger. Baldassare Ceolo,

Superintendent of Police, begged him not to plunge into the back streets and alleys of the old town in search for information, or at least, if he must, to take along two plain-clothes policemen as bodyguards. He was supported in this viewpoint by young Bishop, who as Consul felt at least nominally responsible for Petrosino's safety. The American would have none of it. How was he to do what he had come here to do if he was followed everywhere he went by two great booted policemen who every *picciotto* in Palermo would smell coming at a distance of three miles? No offence meant, of course.

And what exactly was it that he was doing?

If he told them, Petrosino said with a thin smile, it would hardly be a secret, would it?

It wasn't anyway.

Antonio Passananti heard everything that went on within five kilometres of the Quattro Canti, and it became obvious that Petrosino was lining up a team of informers. Bianchi, at the Banca Commerciale, confirmed that the detective was drawing out large sums of money, sometimes two or three hundred lire at a time, and it was not difficult to link these withdrawals with the sudden evidences of comparative wealth among some of the cheaper thugs who roamed the warren of alleys off the Via Papireto or the stews behind the Via della Cala near the port. It was at this point that Don Vito decided he must kill Petrosino.

It was a disinterested decision. Objective. He said so himself. It was simply a matter of prestige, of face. If he let Petrosino continue to do as he wished in Palermo without retaliation, it would imply a softness on his part which he was not prepared to allow. The detective had openly challenged the *alianza* by coming to Sicily to carry out his investigation. It was for the chief of the *alianza* to reply personally. For all the man's blind stupidity, he respected Petrosino's dogged determination and courage. This was not work for some cheap *sicario*.

Passananti demurred, suggesting only that Don Vito had no need to take up this matter personally. It was as close as he dared come to saying that he disagreed. However, Vito Cascio Ferro was prepared to listen no more. Petrosino's affront was no longer tolerable.

It took only a few days to arrange. Certain things had to be set in motion. It was necessary that those with whom Petrosino had spoken, and those others with whom he had made arrangements, should be aware that his death was no casual thing, but a warning which would be as clear as if it had been painted in red letters on the walls of the cathedral. He would die as all classic Mafia victims died: in full view of the world, at high noon, in a public place.

Don Vito was insistent upon the minute observances of the tradition. In the absence of any blood relative, the messenger sent to him was one of his own informers, Carlo Costantino. He was to tell Petrosino, whom he would find at the Tribunale examining records, as he did every morning, that if he was at the corner of the Piazza Marina opposite the Palazzo Partanna, next to the advertising hoarding which carried a poster advertising the appearance that evening of the French comedienne Paule Silver at the Teatro Biondi, he would learn something which would enable him to speedily wind up his work in Palermo and return to America with information which could break the power there of the *alianza*. Naturally, Petrosino would ask for details, and Costantino was to tell him only that the man who was to meet him was the *consigliere* to the *capo dei tutti capi* in Palermo, and that Costantino believed the man was in fear of his life and therefore seeking some kind of arrangement with Petrosino. It was a beautifully baited hook, and Petrosino found it quite irresistible.

He hurried out of the Tribunale and took a horse-cab across town to his hotel. Anxious as he was to make contact with the *mafioso* — Antonio Passananti, Costantino had said he was called — the detective was not going to such a meeting unarmed. He shoved the Smith and Wesson 1902 Military and Police Model into his waistband after checking that five of the six chambers were loaded with the chubby .38 slugs. He came out of the Hotel de France without so much as a sidewalk glance at the Gothic splendour of the Palazzo Chiaramonte to his left, walking purposefully, but not fast. He glanced at his watch: eleven fifty.

Instead of taking the shorter tangent to the left, he walked to the right, a route which would necessitate his going slightly further, but would give him a good deal more time to check the street ahead and behind as he approached the rendezvous.

People were about everywhere, although the *piazza* was not crowded. A group of girls, chattering like starlings, headed for the streetcar waiting at the terminus at the eastern corner of the square. There were one or two sailors in dress-white ogling the girls as they went by from a table outside the Caffe Oreto. The word *Calabria* shone golden from the silken bands on their hats.

Petrosino walked towards the hoarding on the corner. The sun was high now and there was only a little shade beneath the spreading fronds of the huge palms which overhung the railings of the Giardino

Garibaldi. He felt his heart thumping slightly as he discerned a tall, slim, good-looking man, not yet forty, Petrosino judged, standing next to the metal-framed poster hoarding. The man wore a plain dark blue suit and a white shirt, and he looked wary without seeming poised or anxious. His eyes met Petrosino's and did not leave them as the detective came close.

'Lieutenant Petrosino?' His voice was modulated, controlled. 'I am Antonio Passananti.'

He held out his right hand as if it were the most natural thing in the world and Petrosino took it. Passananti's grip was strong, he thought, and then he knew why and he tried to pull free, but the younger man held him that two seconds longer; that two seconds it took for Vito Cascio Ferro to come up behind Petrosino with the French Lebel and fire three of its 8 mm bullets into Petrosino's head and back from a range of less than two feet.

Petrosino was smashed to the ground as Passananti skipped clear, but he was not dead. Astonishingly, impossibly, he was not dead. His right hand moved to the waistband of his trousers, dragging the Smith and Wesson free as Vito Cascio Ferro and Antonio Passananti ran across the street to the Via del Pappagallo, in whose shadows a carriage waited. They were not even across the Piazza when Petrosino's revolver blasted out a single shot. The bullet whined away into infinity off the wall of the church of St Joseph of the Miracles but Petrosino never heard the sound. He lay in a huddled heap on the sidewalk beneath the gay poster advertising Paule Silver, the front of his forehead completely gone, a black pool of arterial blood pumping into the dust-choked gutter where it formed a steadily growing pool.

The first person to venture anywhere near was a young sailor from the *Calabria* named Alberto Cardella. He tried to turn Petrosino's body over, but when he did he had to turn away to be sick. What seemed like much later, the *carabinieri* arrived.

★ ★ ★

The Honourable Michele Ferrantelli had enjoyed his meal.

Don Vito kept a good cook, and her *spaghetto con fungole* were famous in Palermo. Today she was a little cross, because Don Vito had not kept his word to be only fifteen minutes late, and the spaghetti was not the way she like to serve it, just so, *al dente*.

'Tush, tush,' Don Vito had scolded her pleasantly, 'another few minutes — you would not hang me for a few minutes?'

They had settled then to their meal, *pesce arrosto* with fried potatoes, peppered cheese, some fruit, a well-chilled bottle of wine. They talked of many things, of the bright future that lay ahead of Michele now that he was in a place of power, of politics and advancement and the certain things that might be done for a young man with his head screwed on the right way, until Ferrantelli was quite dazzled and had no hesitation in vowing that he would, should the necessity ever arise, swear in any court of law to which he might be summoned that he and Don Vito Cascio Ferro had been together in his house on the Via Archirafi from eleven forty-five that morning until — wait, was it already nearly three? He must no longer trespass on Don Vito's kindness. Well, until three that day, and yes, if Don Vito insisted, another bottle of that good white would be very pleasant, very pleasant indeed.

Vito Cascio Ferro looked up as Passananti appeared in the doorway. 'You will excuse me a moment, my young friend,' he said.

'Of course, of course,' Ferrantelli said, expansively.

Don Vito came into the shadowed hall where Passananti stood waiting. 'Well?'

'His room was searched,' the *consigliere* said. 'You were right.'

'Show me.'

Passananti handed over a sheet of paper. On it, in Petrosino's sloping scrawl, were the words 'Vito Cascio Ferro, born Bisaquino, 22 January 1862, resident Palermo until 1902. Emigrated New York? Present whereabouts? Associates?'

'Burn it,' Don Vito said. 'Anything else?'

'Odds and ends,' Passananti said. 'Nothing important, nothing that need concern you. Oh, and this: I thought you might like to see it.'

His face was as close to a mischievous grin as it could get, and Don Vito frowned, for what Passananti was proferring was a picture postcard. He took it, looked at the picture: Naples. Turning it over, he saw that it was addressed to someone called William Flynn, Department of Justice, Room 804, Custom House, New York City. The message read: 'Am in Palermo. Everything goes well. This is just to send belated thanks — after all, if it hadn't been for you, I'd never have got here. Regards, JP.'

Don Vito looked at his *consigliere* and the same sort of smile touched his bearded mouth. He enjoyed a little irony as much as the next man.

'See that it is mailed,' he said.

Afterword

No one was ever convicted for the murder of Lieutenant Joseph Petrosino, although there were those who said that Commissioner Bingham should have been strung up for giving that story to the newspapers.

In Palermo, Superintendant of Police Ceola, Consul Bishop, Francesco Poli, Commandant of the Mobile Brigade, and the entire Ministry of the Interior, pooled their resources in a campaign to find and convict Petrosino's assassin. Suspicion centred on more than a dozen men, among them Vito Cascio Ferro, Antonio Passananti, and Carlo Costantino. The latter pair had been seen by a workman named Tommaso Chiusa talking in the Giardino Garibaldi the morning of the murder. Unfortunately, neither Costantino and Passananti could be found. They were not at their homes in Partinico. It was suspected that they had left Sicily for the mainland under assumed names. They were never to return.

Vito Cascio Ferro was arrested — in desperation, perhaps — but was able to produce a Deputy named Michele Ferrantelli, patently blameless and demonstrably unconnected with Vito Ferro, who swore that he had been with Don Vito from half an hour before the time of the killing until late in the afternoon. There was nothing that the prosecution could do when the case against Vito Ferro was dismissed 'for lack of evidence.' He lived to be eighty-one years of age, and died in prison where, before he died, he said that, although during his lifetime he had been accused of more than seventy major crimes, twenty of them murders, he had only ever killed one man, and that one quite without malice. The man was, of course, Joseph Petrosino.

A Note to the Reader

There really was a Lieutenant Joseph Petrosino, and much of what you have just read is straight historical fact. However, let me plainly say that I have taken such liberties with history, and with the characters themselves, as I felt necessary in the interests of telling a good story, which is the first duty of the storyteller. However, there really was a William Flynn, there really was a Vito Cascio Ferro, and many of the other characters in the story are from the pages of the past. Petrosino was indeed assassinated in Palermo, and everything he had done to draw attention to the existence of the Mafia was buried with him. Seventy years later, we are, of course, much wiser, as this item from *The Guardian* of 20 March 1974, indicates:

'Nine suspected members of the Mafia were seized in a series of police raids at Palermo and charged with the murder in January of a retired policeman. The policeman, Angelo Sorino, aged 62, had been involved in many anti-Mafia investigations.'

Wherever he is, Don Vito — who enjoyed a little irony as much as the next man — is probably laughing.

FWN 16 April 1974

We do hope that you have enjoyed reading this large print book.

Did you know that all of our titles are available for purchase?

We publish a wide range of high quality large print books including:

Romances, Mysteries, Classics
General Fiction
Non Fiction and Westerns

Special interest titles available in large print are:

The Little Oxford Dictionary
Music Book, Song Book
Hymn Book, Service Book

Also available from us courtesy of Oxford University Press:

Young Readers' Dictionary
(large print edition)
Young Readers' Thesaurus
(large print edition)

For further information or a free brochure, please contact us at:
Ulverscroft Large Print Books Ltd.,
The Green, Bradgate Road, Anstey,
Leicester, LE7 7FU, England.
Tel: (00 44) **0116 236 4325**
Fax: (00 44) **0116 234 0205**

THE ARDAGH EMERALDS

John Hall

England in the 1890s. The world of Victoria and the Empire. This is the world, too, of AJ Raffles, man about town, who, assisted by his inept assistant Bunny Manders, is a successful jewel thief. The eight stories in this book recapture the spirit of the Naughty Nineties, when the gentleman burglar would put out his Sullivan cigarette, don a black mask, outwit a villain, and save a lady in distress — and all before going out to dinner!